Charles Dickens – Out Of Town & Other Short Stories

Charles Dickens (1812-1870) is regarded by many readers and literary critics to be THE major English novelist of the Victorian Age. He is remembered today as the author of a series of weighty novels which have been translated into many languages and promoted to the rank of World Classics. The latter include, but are not limited to, *The Adventures of Oliver Twist*, *A Tale of Two Cities*, *David Copperfield*, *A Christmas Carol*, *Hard Times*, *Great Expectations* and *The Old Curiosity Shop*.

Here we bring you a selection of his quite remarkable short stories.

Contents

The Steam Excursion

Mr. Percy Noakes was a law student, inhabiting a set of chambers on the fourth floor, in one of those houses in Gray's-inn-square which command an extensive view of the gardens, and their usual adjuncts, flaunting nursery-maids, and town-made children, with parenthetical legs. Mr. Percy Noakes was what is generally termed, 'a devilish good fellow.' He had a large circle of acquaintance, and seldom dined at his own expense. He used to talk politics to papas, flatter the vanity of mammas, do the amiable to their daughters, make pleasure engagements with their sons, and romp with the younger branches. Like those paragons of perfection, advertising footmen out of place, he was always 'willing to make himself generally useful.' If any old lady, whose son was in India, gave a ball, Mr. Percy Noakes was master of the ceremonies; if any young lady made a stolen match, Mr. Percy Noakes gave her away; if a juvenile wife presented her husband with a blooming cherub, Mr. Percy Noakes was either godfather, or deputy-godfather; and if any member of a friend's family died, Mr. Percy Noakes was invariably to be seen in the second mourning coach, with a white handkerchief to his eyes, sobbing, to use his own appropriate and expressive description, 'like winkin'!'

It may readily be imagined that these numerous avocations were rather calculated to interfere with Mr. Percy Noakes's professional studies. Mr. Percy Noakes was perfectly aware of the fact, and had, therefore, after mature reflection, made up his mind not to study at all, a laudable determination, to which he adhered in the most praiseworthy manner. His sitting-room presented a strange chaos of dress-gloves, boxing-gloves, caricatures, albums, invitation-cards, foils, cricket-bats, cardboard drawings, paste, gum, and fifty other miscellaneous articles, heaped together in the strangest confusion. He was always making something for somebody, or planning some party of pleasure, which was his great forte. He invariably spoke with astonishing rapidity; was smart, spoffish, and eight-and-twenty.

'Splendid idea, 'pon my life!' soliloquised Mr. Percy Noakes, over his morning coffee, as his mind reverted to a suggestion which had been thrown out on the previous night, by a lady at whose house he had spent the evening. 'Glorious idea! Mrs. Stubbs.'

'Yes, sir,' replied a dirty old woman with an inflamed countenance, emerging from the bedroom, with a barrel of dirt and cinders. This was the laundress. 'Did you call, sir?'

'Oh! Mrs. Stubbs, I'm going out. If that tailor should call again, you'd better say, you'd better say I'm out of town, and shan't be back for a fortnight; and if that bootmaker should come, tell him I've lost his address, or I'd have sent him that little amount. Mind he writes it down; and if Mr. Hardy should call, you know Mr. Hardy?'

'The funny gentleman, sir?'

'Ah! the funny gentleman. If Mr. Hardy should call, say I've gone to Mrs. Taunton's about that water-party.'

'Yes, sir.'

'And if any fellow calls, and says he's come about a steamer, tell him to be here at five o'clock this afternoon, Mrs. Stubbs.'

'Very well, sir.'

Mr. Percy Noakes brushed his hat, whisked the crumbs off his inexpressibles with a silk handkerchief, gave the ends of his hair a persuasive roll round his forefinger, and sallied forth for Mrs. Taunton's domicile in Great Marlborough-street, where she and her daughters occupied the upper part of a house. She was a good- looking widow of fifty, with the form of a giantess and the mind of a child. The pursuit of pleasure, and some means of killing time, were the sole end of her existence. She doted on her daughters, who were as frivolous as herself.

A general exclamation of satisfaction hailed the arrival of Mr. Percy Noakes, who went through the ordinary salutations, and threw himself into an easy chair near the ladies' work-table, with the ease of a regularly established friend of the family. Mrs. Taunton was busily engaged in planting immense bright bows on every part of a smart cap on which it was possible to stick one; Miss Emily Taunton was making a watch-guard; Miss Sophia was at the piano, practising a new song, poetry by the young officer, or the police- officer, or the custom-house officer, or some other interesting amateur.

'You good creature!' said Mrs. Taunton, addressing the gallant Percy. 'You really are a good soul! You've come about the water- party, I know.'

'I should rather suspect I had,' replied Mr. Noakes, triumphantly. 'Now, come here, girls, and I'll tell you all about it.' Miss Emily and Miss Sophia advanced to the table.

'Now,' continued Mr. Percy Noakes, 'it seems to me that the best way will be, to have a committee of ten, to make all the arrangements, and manage the whole set-out. Then, I propose that the expenses shall be paid by these ten fellows jointly.'

'Excellent, indeed!' said Mrs. Taunton, who highly approved of this part of the arrangements.

'Then, my plan is, that each of these ten fellows shall have the power of asking five people. There must be a meeting of the committee, at my chambers, to make all the arrangements, and these people shall be then named; every member of the committee shall have the power of black-balling any one who is proposed; and one black ball shall exclude that person. This will ensure our having a pleasant party, you know.'

'What a manager you are!' interrupted Mrs. Taunton again.

'Charming!' said the lovely Emily.

'I never did!' ejaculated Sophia.

'Yes, I think it'll do,' replied Mr. Percy Noakes, who was now quite in his element. 'I think it'll do. Then you know we shall go down to the Nore, and back, and have a regular capital cold dinner laid out in the cabin before we start, so that everything may be ready without any confusion; and we shall have the lunch laid out, on deck, in those little tea-garden-looking concerns by the paddle-boxes, I don't know what you call 'em. Then, we shall hire a steamer expressly for our party, and a band, and have the deck chalked, and we shall be able to dance quadrilles all day; and then, whoever we know that's musical, you know, why they'll make themselves useful and agreeable; and, and, upon the whole, I really hope we shall have a glorious day, you know!'

The announcement of these arrangements was received with the utmost enthusiasm. Mrs. Taunton, Emily, and Sophia, were loud in their praises.

'Well, but tell me, Percy,' said Mrs. Taunton, 'who are the ten gentlemen to be?'

'Oh! I know plenty of fellows who'll be delighted with the scheme,' replied Mr. Percy Noakes; 'of course we shall have'

'Mr. Hardy!' interrupted the servant, announcing a visitor. Miss Sophia and Miss Emily hastily assumed the most interesting attitudes that could be adopted on so short a notice.

'How are you?' said a stout gentleman of about forty, pausing at the door in the attitude of an awkward harlequin. This was Mr. Hardy, whom we have before described, on the authority of Mrs. Stubbs, as 'the funny gentleman.' He was an Astley-Cooperish Joe Miller, a practical joker, immensely popular with married ladies, and a general favourite with young men. He was always engaged in some pleasure excursion or other, and delighted in getting somebody into a scrape on such occasions. He could sing comic songs, imitate hackney-coachmen and fowls, play airs on his chin, and execute concertos on the Jews'-harp. He always eat and drank most immoderately, and was the bosom friend of Mr. Percy Noakes. He had a red face, a somewhat husky voice, and a tremendous laugh.

'How ARE you?' said this worthy, laughing, as if it were the finest joke in the world to make a morning call, and shaking hands with the ladies with as much vehemence as if their arms had been so many pump-handles.

'You're just the very man I wanted,' said Mr. Percy Noakes, who proceeded to explain the cause of his being in requisition.

'Ha! ha! ha!' shouted Hardy, after hearing the statement, and receiving a detailed account of the proposed excursion. 'Oh, capital! glorious! What a day it will be! what fun! But, I say, when are you going to begin making the arrangements?'

'No time like the present, at once, if you please.'

'Oh, charming!' cried the ladies. 'Pray, do!'

Writing materials were laid before Mr. Percy Noakes, and the names of the different members of the committee were agreed on, after as much discussion between him and Mr. Hardy as if the fate of nations had depended on their appointment. It was then agreed that a meeting should take place at Mr. Percy Noakes's chambers on the ensuing Wednesday evening at eight o'clock, and the visitors departed.

Wednesday evening arrived; eight o'clock came, and eight members of the committee were punctual in their attendance. Mr. Loggins, the solicitor, of Boswell-court, sent an excuse, and Mr. Samuel Briggs, the ditto of Furnival's Inn, sent his brother: much to his (the brother's) satisfaction, and greatly to the discomfiture of Mr. Percy Noakes. Between the Briggses and the Tauntons there existed a degree of implacable hatred, quite unprecedented. The animosity between the Montagues and Capulets, was nothing to that which prevailed between these two illustrious houses. Mrs. Briggs was a widow, with three daughters and two sons; Mr. Samuel, the eldest, was an attorney, and Mr. Alexander, the youngest, was under articles to his brother. They resided in Portland-street, Oxford- street, and moved in the same orbit as the Tauntons, hence their mutual dislike. If the Miss Briggses appeared in smart bonnets, the Miss Tauntons eclipsed them with smarter. If Mrs. Taunton appeared in a cap of all the hues of the rainbow, Mrs. Briggs forthwith mounted a toque, with all the patterns of the kaleidoscope. If Miss Sophia Taunton learnt a new song, two of the Miss Briggses came out with a new duet. The Tauntons had once gained a temporary triumph with the assistance of a harp, but the Briggses brought three guitars into the field, and effectually routed the enemy. There was no end to the rivalry between them.

Now, as Mr. Samuel Briggs was a mere machine, a sort of self-acting legal walking-stick; and as the party was known to have originated, however remotely, with Mrs.

Taunton, the female branches of the Briggs family had arranged that Mr. Alexander should attend, instead of his brother; and as the said Mr. Alexander was deservedly celebrated for possessing all the pertinacity of a bankruptcy-court attorney, combined with the obstinacy of that useful animal which browses on the thistle, he required but little tuition. He was especially enjoined to make himself as disagreeable as possible; and, above all, to black-ball the Tauntons at every hazard.

The proceedings of the evening were opened by Mr. Percy Noakes. After successfully urging on the gentlemen present the propriety of their mixing some brandy-and-water, he briefly stated the object of the meeting, and concluded by observing that the first step must be the selection of a chairman, necessarily possessing some arbitrary, he trusted not unconstitutional, powers, to whom the personal direction of the whole of the arrangements (subject to the approval of the committee) should be confided. A pale young gentleman, in a green stock and spectacles of the same, a member of the honourable society of the Inner Temple, immediately rose for the purpose of proposing Mr. Percy Noakes. He had known him long, and this he would say, that a more honourable, a more excellent, or a better- hearted fellow, never existed. (Hear, hear!) The young gentleman, who was a member of a debating society, took this opportunity of entering into an examination of the state of the English law, from the days of William the Conqueror down to the present period; he briefly adverted to the code established by the ancient Druids; slightly glanced at the principles laid down by the Athenian law- givers; and concluded with a most glowing eulogium on pic-nics and constitutional rights.

Mr. Alexander Briggs opposed the motion. He had the highest esteem for Mr. Percy Noakes as an individual, but he did consider that he ought not to be intrusted with these immense powers (oh, oh!) He believed that in the proposed capacity Mr. Percy Noakes would not act fairly, impartially, or honourably; but he begged it to be distinctly understood, that he said this, without the slightest personal disrespect. Mr. Hardy defended his honourable friend, in a voice rendered partially unintelligible by emotion and brandy- and-water. The proposition was put to the vote, and there appearing to be only one dissentient voice, Mr. Percy Noakes was declared duly elected, and took the chair accordingly.

The business of the meeting now proceeded with rapidity. The chairman delivered in his estimate of the probable expense of the excursion, and every one present subscribed his portion thereof. The question was put that 'The Endeavour' be hired for the occasion; Mr. Alexander Briggs moved as an amendment, that the word 'Fly' be substituted for the word 'Endeavour'; but after some debate consented to withdraw his opposition. The important ceremony of balloting then commenced. A tea-caddy was placed on a table in a dark corner of the apartment, and every one was provided with two backgammon men, one black and one white.

The chairman with great solemnity then read the following list of the guests whom he proposed to introduce:- Mrs. Taunton and two daughters, Mr. Wizzle, Mr. Simson. The names were respectively balloted for, and Mrs. Taunton and her daughters were declared to be black-balled. Mr. Percy Noakes and Mr. Hardy exchanged glances.

'Is your list prepared, Mr. Briggs?' inquired the chairman.

'It is,' replied Alexander, delivering in the following:- 'Mrs. Briggs and three daughters, Mr. Samuel Briggs.' The previous ceremony was repeated, and Mrs. Briggs and three daughters were declared to be black-balled. Mr. Alexander Briggs looked rather foolish, and the remainder of the company appeared somewhat overawed by the mysterious nature of the proceedings.

The balloting proceeded; but, one little circumstance which Mr. Percy Noakes had not originally foreseen, prevented the system from working quite as well as he had anticipated. Everybody was black- balled. Mr. Alexander Briggs, by way of retaliation, exercised his power of exclusion in every instance, and the result was, that after three hours had been consumed in hard balloting, the names of only three gentlemen were found to have been agreed to. In this dilemma what was to be done? either the whole plan must fall to the ground, or a compromise must be effected. The latter alternative was preferable; and Mr. Percy Noakes therefore proposed that the form of balloting should be dispensed with, and that every gentleman should merely be required to state whom he intended to bring. The proposal was acceded to; the Tauntons and the Briggses were reinstated; and the party was formed.

The next Wednesday was fixed for the eventful day, and it was unanimously resolved that every member of the committee should wear a piece of blue sarsenet ribbon round his left arm. It appeared from the statement of Mr. Percy Noakes, that the boat belonged to the General Steam Navigation Company, and was then lying off the Custom-house; and, as he proposed that the dinner and wines should be provided by an eminent city purveyor, it was arranged that Mr. Percy Noakes should be on board by seven o'clock to superintend the arrangements, and that the remaining members of the committee, together with the company generally, should be expected to join her by nine o'clock. More brandy-and-water was despatched; several speeches were made by the different law students present; thanks were voted to the chairman; and the meeting separated.

The weather had been beautiful up to this period, and beautiful it continued to be. Sunday passed over, and Mr. Percy Noakes became unusually fidgety, rushing, constantly, to and from the Steam Packet Wharf, to the astonishment of the clerks, and the great emolument of the Holborn cabmen. Tuesday arrived, and the anxiety of Mr. Percy Noakes knew no bounds. He was every instant running to the window, to look out for clouds; and Mr. Hardy astonished the whole square by practising a new comic song for the occasion, in the chairman's chambers.

Uneasy were the slumbers of Mr. Percy Noakes that night; he tossed and tumbled about, and had confused dreams of steamers starting off, and gigantic clocks with the hands pointing to a quarter-past nine, and the ugly face of Mr. Alexander Briggs looking over the boat's side, and grinning, as if in derision of his fruitless attempts to move. He made a violent effort to get on board, and awoke. The bright sun was shining cheerfully into the bedroom, and Mr. Percy Noakes started up for his watch, in the dreadful expectation of finding his worst dreams realised.

It was just five o'clock. He calculated the time, he should be a good half-hour dressing himself; and as it was a lovely morning, and the tide would be then running down, he would walk leisurely to Strand-lane, and have a boat to the Custom-house.

He dressed himself, took a hasty apology for a breakfast, and sallied forth. The streets looked as lonely and deserted as if they had been crowded, overnight, for the last time. Here and there, an early apprentice, with quenched-looking sleepy eyes, was taking down the shutters of a shop; and a policeman or milkwoman might occasionally be seen pacing slowly along; but the servants had not yet begun to clean the doors, or light the kitchen fires, and London looked the picture of desolation. At the corner of a by-street, near Temple-bar, was stationed a 'street-breakfast.' The coffee was boiling over a charcoal fire, and large slices of bread and butter were piled one upon the other, like deals in a timber-yard. The company were seated on a form, which, with a view both to security and comfort, was placed against a neighbouring wall. Two young men, whose uproarious mirth and disordered dress bespoke the conviviality of the preceding evening, were treating three 'ladies' and an Irish labourer. A little sweep was standing at a short distance, casting a longing eye at the tempting delicacies; and a policeman was watching the group from the opposite side of the street. The wan looks and gaudy finery of the thinly-clad women contrasted as strangely with the gay sunlight, as did their forced merriment with the boisterous hilarity of the two young men, who, now and then, varied their amusements by 'bonneting' the proprietor of this itinerant coffee-house.

Mr. Percy Noakes walked briskly by, and when he turned down Strand- lane, and caught a glimpse of the glistening water, he thought he had never felt so important or so happy in his life.

'Boat, sir?' cried one of the three watermen who were mopping out their boats, and all whistling. 'Boat, sir?'

'No,' replied Mr. Percy Noakes, rather sharply; for the inquiry was not made in a manner at all suitable to his dignity.

'Would you prefer a wessel, sir?' inquired another, to the infinite delight of the 'Jack-in-the-water.'

Mr. Percy Noakes replied with a look of supreme contempt.

'Did you want to be put on board a steamer, sir?' inquired an old fireman-waterman, very confidentially. He was dressed in a faded red suit, just the colour of the cover of a very old Court-guide.

'Yes, make haste, the Endeavour, off the Custom-house.'

'Endeavour!' cried the man who had convulsed the 'Jack' before. 'Vy, I see the Endeavour go up half an hour ago.'

'So did I,' said another; 'and I should think she'd gone down by this time, for she's a precious sight too full of ladies and gen'lemen.'

Mr. Percy Noakes affected to disregard these representations, and stepped into the boat, which the old man, by dint of scrambling, and shoving, and grating, had brought up to the causeway. 'Shove her off!' cried Mr. Percy Noakes, and away the boat glided down the river; Mr. Percy Noakes seated on the recently mopped seat, and the watermen at the stairs offering to bet him any reasonable sum that he'd never reach the 'Custum-us.'

'Here she is, by Jove!' said the delighted Percy, as they ran alongside the Endeavour.

'Hold hard!' cried the steward over the side, and Mr. Percy Noakes jumped on board.

'Hope you will find everything as you wished, sir. She looks uncommon well this morning.'

'She does, indeed,' replied the manager, in a state of ecstasy which it is impossible to describe. The deck was scrubbed, and the seats were scrubbed, and there was a bench for the band, and a place for dancing, and a pile of camp-stools, and an awning; and then Mr. Percy Noakes bustled down below, and there were the pastrycook's men, and the steward's wife, laying out the dinner on two tables the whole length of the cabin; and then Mr. Percy Noakes took off his coat and rushed backwards and forwards, doing nothing, but quite convinced he was assisting everybody; and the steward's wife laughed till she cried, and Mr. Percy Noakes panted with the violence of his exertions. And then the bell at London-bridge wharf rang; and a Margate boat was just starting; and a Gravesend boat was just starting, and people shouted, and porters ran down the steps with luggage that would crush any men but porters; and sloping boards, with bits of wood nailed on them, were placed between the outside boat and the inside boat; and the passengers ran along them, and looked like so many fowls coming out of an area; and then, the bell ceased, and the boards were taken away, and the boats started, and the whole scene was one of the most delightful bustle and confusion.

The time wore on; half-past eight o'clock arrived; the pastry- cook's men went ashore; the dinner was completely laid out; and Mr. Percy Noakes locked the principal cabin, and put the key in his pocket, in order that it might be suddenly disclosed, in all its magnificence, to the eyes of the astonished company. The band came on board, and so did the wine.

Ten minutes to nine, and the committee embarked in a body. There was Mr. Hardy, in a blue jacket and waistcoat, white trousers, silk stockings, and pumps, in full aquatic costume, with a straw hat on his head, and an immense telescope under his arm; and there was the young gentleman with the green spectacles, in nankeen inexplicables, with a ditto waistcoat and bright buttons, like the pictures of Paul, not the saint, but he of Virginia notoriety. The remainder of the committee, dressed in white hats, light jackets, waistcoats, and trousers, looked something between waiters and West India planters.

Nine o'clock struck, and the company arrived in shoals. Mr. Samuel Briggs, Mrs. Briggs, and the Misses Briggs, made their appearance in a smart private wherry. The three guitars, in their respective dark green cases, were carefully stowed away in the bottom of the boat, accompanied by two immense portfolios of music, which it would take at least a week's incessant playing to get through. The Tauntons arrived at the same moment with more music, and a lion, a gentleman with a bass voice and an incipient red moustache. The colours of the Taunton party were pink; those of the Briggses a light blue. The Tauntons had artificial flowers in their bonnets; here the Briggses gained a decided advantage, they wore feathers.

'How d'ye do, dear?' said the Misses Briggs to the Misses Taunton. (The word 'dear' among girls is frequently synonymous with 'wretch.')

'Quite well, thank you, dear,' replied the Misses Taunton to the Misses Briggs; and then, there was such a kissing, and congratulating, and shaking of hands, as might have induced one to suppose that the two families were the best friends in the world, instead of each wishing the other overboard, as they most sincerely did.

Mr. Percy Noakes received the visitors, and bowed to the strange gentleman, as if he should like to know who he was. This was just what Mrs. Taunton wanted. Here was an opportunity to astonish the Briggses.

'Oh! I beg your pardon,' said the general of the Taunton party, with a careless air. 'Captain Helves, Mr. Percy Noakes, Mrs. Briggs, Captain Helves.'

Mr. Percy Noakes bowed very low; the gallant captain did the same with all due ferocity, and the Briggses were clearly overcome.

'Our friend, Mr. Wizzle, being unfortunately prevented from coming,' resumed Mrs. Taunton, 'I did myself the pleasure of bringing the captain, whose musical talents I knew would be a great acquisition.'

'In the name of the committee I have to thank you for doing so, and to offer you welcome, sir,' replied Percy. (Here the scraping was renewed.) 'But pray be seated, won't you walk aft? Captain, will you conduct Miss Taunton? Miss Briggs, will you allow me?'

'Where could they have picked up that military man?' inquired Mrs. Briggs of Miss Kate Briggs, as they followed the little party.

'I can't imagine,' replied Miss Kate, bursting with vexation; for the very fierce air with which the gallant captain regarded the company, had impressed her with a high sense of his importance.

Boat after boat came alongside, and guest after guest arrived. The invites had been excellently arranged: Mr. Percy Noakes having considered it as important that the number of young men should exactly tally with that of the young ladies, as that the quantity of knives on board should be in precise proportion to the forks.

'Now, is every one on board?' inquired Mr. Percy Noakes. The committee (who, with their bits of blue ribbon, looked as if they were all going to be bled) bustled about to ascertain the fact, and reported that they might safely start.

'Go on!' cried the master of the boat from the top of one of the paddle-boxes.

'Go on!' echoed the boy, who was stationed over the hatchway to pass the directions down to the engineer; and away went the vessel with that agreeable noise which is peculiar to steamers, and which is composed of a mixture of creaking, gushing, clanging, and snorting.

'Hoi-oi-oi-oi-oi-oi-o-i-i-i!' shouted half-a-dozen voices from a boat, a quarter of a mile astern.

'Ease her!' cried the captain: 'do these people belong to us, sir?'

'Noakes,' exclaimed Hardy, who had been looking at every object far and near, through the large telescope, 'it's the Fleetwoods and the Wakefields and two children with them, by Jove!'

'What a shame to bring children!' said everybody; 'how very inconsiderate!'

'I say, it would be a good joke to pretend not to see 'em, wouldn't it?' suggested Hardy, to the immense delight of the company generally. A council of war was hastily held, and it was resolved that the newcomers should be taken on board, on Mr. Hardy solemnly pledging himself to tease the children during the whole of the day.

'Stop her!' cried the captain.

'Stop her!' repeated the boy; whizz went the steam, and all the young ladies, as in duty bound, screamed in concert. They were only appeased by the assurance of the martial Helves, that the escape of steam consequent on stopping a vessel was seldom attended with any great loss of human life.

Two men ran to the side; and after some shouting, and swearing, and angling for the wherry with a boat-hook, Mr. Fleetwood, and Mrs. Fleetwood, and Master Fleetwood, and Mr. Wakefield, and Mrs. Wakefield, and Miss Wakefield, were safely deposited on the deck. The girl was about six years old, the boy about four; the former was dressed in a white frock with a pink sash and dog's-eared- looking little spencer: a straw bonnet and green veil, six inches by three and a half; the latter, was attired for the occasion in a nankeen frock, between the bottom of which, and the top of his plaid socks, a considerable portion of two small mottled legs was discernible. He had a light blue cap with a gold band and tassel on his head, and a damp piece of gingerbread in his hand, with which he had slightly embossed his countenance.

The boat once more started off; the band played 'Off she goes:' the major part of the company conversed cheerfully in groups; and the old gentlemen walked up and down the deck in pairs, as perseveringly and gravely as if they were doing a match against time for an immense stake. They ran briskly down the Pool; the gentlemen pointed out the Docks, the Thames Police-office, and other elegant public edifices; and the young ladies exhibited a proper display of horror at the appearance of the coal-whippers and ballast-heavers. Mr. Hardy told stories to the married ladies, at which they laughed very much in their pocket-handkerchiefs, and hit him on the knuckles with their fans, declaring him to be 'a naughty man, a shocking creature', and so forth; and Captain Helves gave slight descriptions of battles and duels, with a most bloodthirsty air, which made him the admiration of the women, and the envy of the men. Quadrilling commenced; Captain Helves danced one set with Miss Emily

Taunton, and another set with Miss Sophia Taunton. Mrs. Taunton was in ecstasies. The victory appeared to be complete; but alas! the inconstancy of man! Having performed this necessary duty, he attached himself solely to Miss Julia Briggs, with whom he danced no less than three sets consecutively, and from whose side he evinced no intention of stirring for the remainder of the day.

Mr. Hardy, having played one or two very brilliant fantasias on the Jews'-harp, and having frequently repeated the exquisitely amusing joke of slily chalking a large cross on the back of some member of the committee, Mr. Percy Noakes expressed his hope that some of their musical friends would oblige the company by a display of their abilities.

'Perhaps,' he said in a very insinuating manner, 'Captain Helves will oblige us?' Mrs. Taunton's countenance lighted up, for the captain only sang duets, and couldn't sing them with anybody but one of her daughters.

'Really,' said that warlike individual, 'I should be very happy, 'but'

'Oh! pray do,' cried all the young ladies.

'Miss Emily, have you any objection to join in a duet?'

'Oh! not the slightest,' returned the young lady, in a tone which clearly showed she had the greatest possible objection.

'Shall I accompany you, dear?' inquired one of the Miss Briggses, with the bland intention of spoiling the effect.

'Very much obliged to you, Miss Briggs,' sharply retorted Mrs. Taunton, who saw through the manoeuvre; 'my daughters always sing without accompaniments.'

'And without voices,' tittered Mrs. Briggs, in a low tone.

'Perhaps,' said Mrs. Taunton, reddening, for she guessed the tenor of the observation, though she had not heard it clearly 'Perhaps it would be as well for some people, if their voices were not quite so audible as they are to other people.'

'And, perhaps, if gentlemen who are kidnapped to pay attention to some persons' daughters, had not sufficient discernment to pay attention to other persons' daughters,' returned Mrs. Briggs, 'some persons would not be so ready to display that ill-temper which, thank God, distinguishes them from other persons.'

'Persons!' ejaculated Mrs. Taunton.

'Persons,' replied Mrs. Briggs.

'Insolence!'

'Creature!'

'Hush! hush!' interrupted Mr. Percy Noakes, who was one of the very few by whom this dialogue had been overheard. 'Hush! pray, silence for the duet.'

After a great deal of preparatory crowing and humming, the captain began the following duet from the opera of 'Paul and Virginia,' in that grunting tone in which a man gets down, Heaven knows where, without the remotest chance of ever getting up again. This, in private circles, is frequently designated 'a bass voice.'

'See (sung the captain) from o-ce-an ri-sing Bright flames the or-b of d-ay. From yon gro-ove, the varied so-ongs'

Here, the singer was interrupted by varied cries of the most dreadful description, proceeding from some grove in the immediate vicinity of the starboard paddle-box.

'My child!' screamed Mrs. Fleetwood. 'My child! it is his voice, I know it.'

Mr. Fleetwood, accompanied by several gentlemen, here rushed to the quarter from whence the noise proceeded, and an exclamation of horror burst from the company; the general impression being, that the little innocent had either got his head in the water, or his legs in the machinery.

'What is the matter?' shouted the agonised father, as he returned with the child in his arms.

'Oh! oh! oh!' screamed the small sufferer again.

'What is the matter, dear?' inquired the father once more, hastily stripping off the nankeen frock, for the purpose of ascertaining whether the child had one bone which was not smashed to pieces.

'Oh! oh! I'm so frightened!'

'What at, dear? what at?' said the mother, soothing the sweet infant.

'Oh! he's been making such dreadful faces at me,' cried the boy, relapsing into convulsions at the bare recollection.

'He! who?' cried everybody, crowding round him.

'Oh! him!' replied the child, pointing at Hardy, who affected to be the most concerned of the whole group.

The real state of the case at once flashed upon the minds of all present, with the exception of the Fleetwoods and the Wakefields. The facetious Hardy, in fulfilment of his promise, had watched the child to a remote part of the vessel, and, suddenly appearing before him with the most awful contortions of visage, had produced his paroxysm of terror. Of course, he now observed that it was hardly necessary for him to deny the accusation; and the unfortunate little victim was accordingly led below, after receiving sundry thumps on the head from both his parents, for having the wickedness to tell a story.

This little interruption having been adjusted, the captain resumed, and Miss Emily chimed in, in due course. The duet was loudly applauded, and, certainly, the perfect independence of the parties deserved great commendation. Miss Emily sung her part, without the slightest reference to the captain; and the captain sang so loud, that he had not the slightest idea what was being done by his partner. After having gone through the last few eighteen or nineteen bars by himself, therefore, he acknowledged the plaudits of the circle with that air of self-denial which men usually assume when they think they have done something to astonish the company.

'Now,' said Mr. Percy Noakes, who had just ascended from the fore- cabin, where he had been busily engaged in decanting the wine, 'if the Misses Briggs will oblige us with something before dinner, I am sure we shall be very much delighted.'

One of those hums of admiration followed the suggestion, which one frequently hears in society, when nobody has the most distant notion what he is expressing his approval of. The three Misses Briggs looked modestly at their mamma, and the mamma looked approvingly at her daughters, and Mrs. Taunton looked scornfully at all of them. The Misses Briggs asked for their guitars, and several gentlemen seriously damaged the cases in their anxiety to present them. Then, there was a very interesting production of three little keys for the aforesaid cases, and a melodramatic expression of horror at finding a string broken; and a vast deal of screwing and tightening, and winding, and tuning, during which Mrs. Briggs expatiated to those near her on the immense difficulty of playing a guitar, and hinted at the wondrous proficiency of her daughters in that mystic art. Mrs. Taunton whispered to a neighbour that it was 'quite sickening!' and the Misses Taunton looked as if they knew how to play, but disdained to do it.

At length, the Misses Briggs began in real earnest. It was a new Spanish composition, for three voices and three guitars. The effect was electrical. All eyes were turned upon the captain, who was reported to have once passed through Spain with his regiment, and who must be well acquainted with the national music. He was in raptures. This was sufficient; the trio was encored; the applause was universal; and never had the Tauntons suffered such a complete defeat.

'Bravo! bravo!' ejaculated the captain; 'bravo!'

'Pretty! isn't it, sir?' inquired Mr. Samuel Briggs, with the air of a self-satisfied showman. By-the-bye, these were the first words he had been heard to utter since he left Boswell-court the evening before.

'De-lightful!' returned the captain, with a flourish, and a military cough; 'de-lightful!'

'Sweet instrument!' said an old gentleman with a bald head, who had been trying all the morning to look through a telescope, inside the glass of which Mr. Hardy had fixed a large black wafer.

'Did you ever hear a Portuguese tambourine?' inquired that jocular individual.

'Did YOU ever hear a tom-tom, sir?' sternly inquired the captain, who lost no opportunity of showing off his travels, real or pretended.

'A what?' asked Hardy, rather taken aback.

'A tom-tom.'

'Never!'

'Nor a gum-gum?'

'Never!'

'What IS a gum-gum?' eagerly inquired several young ladies.

'When I was in the East Indies,' replied the captain (here was a discovery, he had been in the East Indies!) 'when I was in the East Indies, I was once stopping a few thousand miles up the country, on a visit at the house of a very particular friend of mine, Ram Chowdar Doss Azuph Al Bowlar, a devilish pleasant fellow. As we were enjoying our hookahs, one evening, in the cool verandah in front of his villa, we were rather surprised by the sudden appearance of thirty-four of his Kit-ma-gars (for he had rather a large establishment there), accompanied by an equal number of Con- su-mars, approaching the house with a threatening aspect, and beating a tom-tom. The Ram started up'

'Who?' inquired the bald gentleman, intensely interested.

'The Ram, Ram Chowdar'

'Oh!' said the old gentleman, 'beg your pardon; pray go on.'

'Started up and drew a pistol. "Helves," said he, "my boy," he always called me, my boy "Helves," said he, "do you hear that tom- tom?" "I do," said I. His countenance, which before was pale, assumed a most frightful appearance; his whole visage was distorted, and his frame shaken by violent emotions. "Do you see that gum-gum?" said he. "No," said I, staring about me. "You don't?" said he. "No, I'll be damned if I do," said I; "and what's more, I don't know what a gum-gum is," said I. I really thought the Ram would have dropped. He drew me aside, and with an expression of agony I shall never forget, said in a low whisper'

'Dinner's on the table, ladies,' interrupted the steward's wife.

'Will you allow me?' said the captain, immediately suiting the action to the word, and escorting Miss Julia Briggs to the cabin, with as much ease as if he had finished the story.

'What an extraordinary circumstance!' ejaculated the same old gentleman, preserving his listening attitude.

'What a traveller!' said the young ladies.

'What a singular name!' exclaimed the gentlemen, rather confused by the coolness of the whole affair.

'I wish he had finished the story,' said an old lady. 'I wonder what a gum-gum really is?'

'By Jove!' exclaimed Hardy, who until now had been lost in utter amazement, 'I don't know what it may be in India, but in England I think a gum-gum has very much the same meaning as a hum-bug.'

'How illiberal! how envious!' cried everybody, as they made for the cabin, fully impressed with a belief in the captain's amazing adventures. Helves was the sole lion for the remainder of the day, impudence and the marvellous are pretty sure passports to any society.

The party had by this time reached their destination, and put about on their return home. The wind, which had been with them the whole day, was now directly in their teeth; the weather had become gradually more and more overcast; and the sky, water, and shore, were all of that dull, heavy, uniform lead-colour, which house-painters daub in the first instance over a street-door which is gradually approaching a state of convalescence. It had been 'spitting' with rain for the last half-hour, and now began to pour in good earnest. The wind was freshening very fast, and the waterman at the wheel had unequivocally expressed his opinion that there would shortly be a squall. A slight emotion on the part of the vessel, now and then, seemed to suggest the possibility of its pitching to a very uncomfortable extent in the event of its blowing harder; and every timber began to creak, as if the boat were an overladen clothes-basket. Sea-sickness, however, is like a belief in ghosts, every one entertains some misgivings on the subject, but few will acknowledge any. The majority of the company, therefore, endeavoured to look peculiarly happy, feeling all the while especially miserable.

'Don't it rain?' inquired the old gentleman before noticed, when, by dint of squeezing and jamming, they were all seated at table.

'I think it does, a little,' replied Mr. Percy Noakes, who could hardly hear himself speak, in consequence of the pattering on the deck.

'Don't it blow?' inquired some one else.

'No, I don't think it does,' responded Hardy, sincerely wishing that he could persuade himself that it did not; for he sat near the door, and was almost blown off his seat.

'It'll soon clear up,' said Mr. Percy Noakes, in a cheerful tone.

'Oh, certainly!' ejaculated the committee generally.

'No doubt of it!' said the remainder of the company, whose attention was now pretty well engrossed by the serious business of eating, carving, taking wine, and so forth.

The throbbing motion of the engine was but too perceptible. There was a large, substantial, cold boiled leg of mutton, at the bottom of the table, shaking like blancmange; a previously hearty sirloin of beef looked as if it had been suddenly seized with the palsy; and some tongues, which were placed on dishes rather too large for them, went through the most surprising evolutions; darting from side to side, and from end to end, like a fly in an inverted wine- glass. Then, the sweets shook and trembled, till it was quite impossible to help them, and people gave up the attempt in despair; and the pigeon-pies looked as if the birds, whose legs were stuck outside, were trying to get them in. The table vibrated and started like a feverish pulse, and the very legs were convulsed, everything was shaking and jarring. The beams in the roof of the cabin seemed as if they were put there for the sole purpose of giving people head-aches, and several elderly gentlemen became ill-tempered in consequence. As fast as the steward put the fire-irons up, they WOULD fall down again; and the more the ladies and gentlemen tried to sit comfortably on their seats, the more the seats seemed to slide away from the ladies and gentlemen. Several ominous demands were made for small glasses of brandy; the countenances of the company gradually underwent most extraordinary changes; one gentleman was observed suddenly to rush from table without the slightest ostensible reason, and dart up the steps with incredible swiftness: thereby greatly damaging both himself and the steward, who happened to be coming down at the same moment.

The cloth was removed; the dessert was laid on the table; and the glasses were filled. The motion of the boat increased; several members of the party began to feel rather vague and misty, and looked as if they had only just got up. The young gentleman with the spectacles, who had been in a fluctuating state for some time, at one moment bright, and at another dismal, like a revolving light on the sea-coast, rashly announced his wish to propose a toast. After several ineffectual attempts to preserve his perpendicular, the young gentleman, having managed to hook himself to the centre leg of the table with his left hand, proceeded as follows:

'Ladies and gentlemen. A gentleman is among us, I may say a stranger (here some painful thought seemed to strike the orator; he paused, and looked extremely odd) whose talents, whose travels, whose cheerfulness'

'I beg your pardon, Edkins,' hastily interrupted Mr. Percy Noakes, 'Hardy, what's the matter?'

'Nothing,' replied the 'funny gentleman,' who had just life enough left to utter two consecutive syllables.

'Will you have some brandy?'

'No!' replied Hardy in a tone of great indignation, and looking as comfortable as Temple-bar in a Scotch mist; 'what should I want brandy for?'

'Will you go on deck?'

'No, I will NOT.' This was said with a most determined air, and in a voice which might have been taken for an imitation of anything; it was quite as much like a guinea-pig as a bassoon.

'I beg your pardon, Edkins,' said the courteous Percy; 'I thought our friend was ill. Pray go on.'

A pause.

'Pray go on.'

'Mr. Edkins IS gone,' cried somebody.

'I beg your pardon, sir,' said the steward, running up to Mr. Percy Noakes, 'I beg your pardon, sir, but the gentleman as just went on deck, him with the green spectacles, is uncommon bad, to be sure; and the young man as played the wiolin says, that unless he has some brandy he can't answer for the consequences. He says he has a wife and two children, whose werry subsistence depends on his breaking a wessel, and he expects to do so every moment. The flageolet's been werry ill, but he's better, only he's in a dreadful prusperation.'

All disguise was now useless; the company staggered on deck; the gentlemen tried to see nothing but the clouds; and the ladies, muffled up in such shawls and cloaks as they had brought with them, lay about on the seats, and under the seats, in the most wretched condition. Never was such a blowing, and raining, and pitching, and tossing, endured by any pleasure party before. Several remonstrances were sent down below, on the subject of Master Fleetwood, but they were totally unheeded in consequence of the indisposition of his natural protectors. That interesting child screamed at the top of his voice, until he had no voice left to scream with; and then, Miss Wakefield began, and screamed for the remainder of the passage.

Mr. Hardy was observed, some hours afterwards, in an attitude which induced his friends to suppose that he was busily engaged in contemplating the beauties of the deep; they only regretted that his taste for the picturesque should lead him to remain so long in a position, very injurious at all times, but especially so, to an individual labouring under a tendency of blood to the head.

The party arrived off the Custom-house at about two o'clock on the Thursday morning dispirited and worn out. The Tauntons were too ill to quarrel with the Briggses, and the Briggses were too wretched to annoy the Tauntons. One of the guitar-cases was lost on its passage to a hackney-coach, and Mrs. Briggs has not scrupled to state that the Tauntons bribed a porter to throw it down an area. Mr. Alexander Briggs opposes vote by ballot, he says from personal experience of its inefficacy; and Mr. Samuel Briggs, whenever he is asked to express his sentiments on the point, says he has no opinion on that or any other subject.

Mr. Edkins, the young gentleman in the green spectacles, makes a speech on every occasion on which a speech can possibly be made: the eloquence of which can only be equalled by its length. In the event of his not being previously appointed to a judgeship, it is probable that he will practise as a barrister in the New Central Criminal Court.

Captain Helves continued his attention to Miss Julia Briggs, whom he might possibly have espoused, if it had not unfortunately happened that Mr. Samuel arrested him, in the way of business, pursuant to instructions received from Messrs. Scroggins and Payne, whose town-debts the gallant captain had condescended to collect, but whose accounts, with the indiscretion sometimes peculiar to military minds, he had omitted to keep with that dull accuracy which custom has rendered necessary. Mrs. Taunton complains that she has been much deceived in him. He introduced himself to the family on board a Gravesend steam-packet, and certainly, therefore, ought to have proved respectable.

Mr. Percy Noakes is as light-hearted and careless as ever.

Out of Town

Sitting, on a bright September morning, among my books and papers at my open window on the cliff overhanging the sea-beach, I have the sky and ocean framed before me like a beautiful picture. A beautiful picture, but with such movement in it, such changes of light upon the sails of ships and wake of steamboats, such dazzling gleams of silver far out at sea, such fresh touches on the crisp wave-tops as they break and roll towards me - a picture with such music in the billowy rush upon the shingle, the blowing of morning wind through the corn-sheaves where the farmers' waggons are busy, the singing of the larks, and the distant voices of children at play - such charms of sight and sound as all the Galleries on earth can but poorly suggest.

So dreamy is the murmur of the sea below my window, that I may have been here, for anything I know, one hundred years. Not that I have grown old, for, daily on the neighbouring downs and grassy hill- sides, I find that I can still in reason walk any distance, jump over anything, and climb up anywhere; but, that the sound of the ocean seems to have become so customary to my musings, and other realities seem so to have gone aboard ship and floated away over the horizon, that, for aught I will undertake to the contrary, I am the enchanted son of the King my father, shut up in a tower on the sea-shore, for protection against an old she-goblin who insisted on being my godmother, and who foresaw at the font - wonderful creature! - that I should get into a scrape before I was twenty- one. I remember to have been in a City (my Royal parent's dominions, I suppose), and apparently not long ago either, that was in the dreariest condition. The principal inhabitants had all been changed into old newspapers, and in that form were preserving their window-blinds from dust, and wrapping all their smaller household gods in curl-papers. I walked through gloomy streets where every house was shut up and newspapered, and where my solitary footsteps echoed on the deserted pavements. In the public rides there were no carriages, no horses, no animated existence, but a few sleepy policemen, and a few adventurous boys taking advantage of the devastation to swarm up the lamp-posts. In the Westward streets there was no traffic; in the Westward shops, no business. The water-patterns which the 'Prentices had trickled out on the pavements early in the morning, remained uneffaced by human feet. At the corners of mews, Cochin-China fowls stalked gaunt and savage; nobody being left in the deserted city (as it appeared to me), to feed them. Public Houses, where splendid footmen swinging their legs over gorgeous hammer-cloths beside wigged coachmen were wont to regale, were silent, and the unused pewter pots shone, too bright for business, on the shelves. I beheld a Punch's Show leaning against a wall near Park Lane, as if it had fainted. It was deserted, and there were none to heed its desolation. In Belgrave Square I met the last man - an ostler - sitting on a post in a ragged red waistcoat, eating straw, and mildewing away.

If I recollect the name of the little town, on whose shore this sea is murmuring - but I am not just now, as I have premised, to be relied upon for anything - it is Pavilionstone. Within a quarter of a century, it was a little fishing town, and they do say, that the time was, when it was a little smuggling town. I have heard that it was rather famous in the hollands and brandy way, and that coevally with that reputation the lamplighter's was considered a bad life at the Assurance Offices. It was observed that if he were not particular about lighting up, he lived in peace; but that, if he made the best of the oil-lamps in the steep and narrow streets, he usually fell over the cliff at an early age. Now, gas and electricity run to the very water's edge, and the South-Eastern Railway Company screech at us in the dead of night.

But, the old little fishing and smuggling town remains, and is so tempting a place for the latter purpose, that I think of going out some night next week, in a fur cap and a pair of petticoat trousers, and running an empty tub, as a kind of archaeological pursuit. Let nobody with corns come to Pavilionstone, for there are breakneck flights of ragged steps, connecting the principal streets by back-ways, which will cripple that visitor in half an hour. These are the ways by which, when I run that tub, I shall escape. I shall make a Thermopylae of the corner of one of them, defend it with my cutlass against the coast-guard until my brave companions have sheered off, then dive into the darkness, and regain my Susan's arms. In connection with these breakneck steps I observe some wooden cottages, with tumble-down out-houses, and back-yards three feet square, adorned with garlands of dried fish, in one of which (though the General Board of Health might object) my Susan dwells.

The South-Eastern Company have brought Pavilionstone into such vogue, with their tidal trains and splendid steam-packets, that a new Pavilionstone is rising up. I am, myself, of New Pavilionstone. We are a little mortary and limey at present, but we are getting on capitally. Indeed, we were getting on so fast, at one time, that we rather overdid it, and built a street of shops, the business of which may be expected to arrive in about ten years. We are sensibly laid out in general; and with a little care and pains (by no means wanting, so far), shall become a very pretty place. We ought to be, for our situation is delightful, our air is delicious, and our breezy hills and downs, carpeted with wild thyme, and decorated with millions of wild flowers, are, on the faith of a pedestrian, perfect. In New Pavilionstone we are a little too much addicted to small windows with more bricks in them than glass, and we are not over-fanciful in the way of decorative architecture, and we get unexpected sea-views through cracks in the street doors; on the whole, however, we are very snug and comfortable, and well accommodated. But the Home Secretary (if there be such an officer) cannot too soon shut up the burial-ground of the old parish church. It is in the midst of us, and Pavilionstone will get no good of it, if it be too long left alone.

The lion of Pavilionstone is its Great Hotel. A dozen years ago, going over to Paris by South-Eastern Tidal Steamer, you used to be dropped upon the platform of the main line Pavilionstone Station (not a junction then), at eleven o'clock on a dark winter's night, in a roaring wind; and in the howling wilderness outside the station, was a short omnibus which brought you up by the forehead the instant you got in at the door; and nobody cared about you, and you were alone in the world. You bumped over infinite chalk, until you were turned out at a strange building which had just left off being a barn without having quite begun to be a house, where nobody expected your coming, or knew what to do with you when you were come, and where you were usually blown about, until you happened to be blown against the cold beef, and finally into bed. At five in the morning you were blown out of bed, and after a dreary breakfast, with crumpled company, in the midst of confusion, were hustled on board a steamboat and lay wretched on deck until you saw France lunging and surging at you with great vehemence over the bowsprit.

Now, you come down to Pavilionstone in a free and easy manner, an irresponsible agent, made over in trust to the South-Eastern Company, until you get out of the railway-carriage at high-water mark. If you are crossing by the boat at once, you have nothing to do but walk on board and be happy there if you can - I can't. If you are going to our Great Pavilionstone Hotel, the sprightliest porters under the sun, whose cheerful looks are a pleasant welcome, shoulder your luggage, drive it off in vans, bowl it away in trucks, and enjoy themselves in playing athletic games with it. If you are for public life at our great Pavilionstone Hotel, you walk into that establishment as if it were your club; and find ready for you, your news-room, dining-room, smoking-room, billiard-room, music-room, public breakfast, public dinner twice a-day (one plain, one gorgeous), hot baths and cold baths. If you want to be bored, there are plenty of bores always ready for you, and from Saturday to Monday in particular, you can be bored (if you like it) through and through. Should you want to be private at our Great Pavilionstone Hotel, say but the word, look at the list of charges, choose your floor, name your figure - there you are, established in your castle, by the day, week, month, or year, innocent of all comers or goers, unless you have my fancy for walking early in the morning down the groves of boots and shoes, which so regularly flourish at all the chamber-doors before breakfast, that it seems to me as if nobody ever got up or took them in. Are you going across the Alps, and would you like to air your Italian at our Great Pavilionstone Hotel? Talk to the Manager - always conversational, accomplished, and polite. Do you want to be aided, abetted, comforted, or advised, at our Great Pavilionstone Hotel? Send for the good landlord, and he is your friend. Should you, or any one belonging to you, ever be taken ill at our Great Pavilionstone Hotel, you will not soon forget him or his kind wife. And when you pay your bill at our Great Pavilionstone Hotel, you will not be put out of humour by anything you find in it.

A thoroughly good inn, in the days of coaching and posting, was a noble place. But no such inn would have been equal to the reception of four or five hundred people, all of them wet through, and half of them dead sick, every day in the year. This is where we shine, in our Pavilionstone Hotel. Again - who, coming and going, pitching and tossing, boating and training, hurrying in, and flying out, could ever have calculated the fees to be paid at an old-fashioned house? In our Pavilionstone Hotel vocabulary, there is no such word as fee. Everything is done for you; every service is provided at a fixed and reasonable charge; all the prices are hung up in all the rooms; and you can make out your own bill beforehand, as well as the book-keeper.

In the case of your being a pictorial artist, desirous of studying at small expense the physiognomies and beards of different nations, come, on receipt of this, to Pavilionstone. You shall find all the nations of the earth, and all the styles of shaving and not shaving, hair cutting and hair letting alone, for ever flowing through our hotel. Couriers you shall see by hundreds; fat leathern bags for five-franc pieces, closing with violent snaps, like discharges of fire-arms, by thousands; more luggage in a morning than, fifty years ago, all Europe saw in a week. Looking at trains, steamboats, sick travellers, and luggage, is our great Pavilionstone recreation. We are not strong in other public amusements. We have a Literary and Scientific

Institution, and we have a Working Men's Institution - may it hold many gipsy holidays in summer fields, with the kettle boiling, the band of music playing, and the people dancing; and may I be on the hill-side, looking on with pleasure at a wholesome sight too rare in England! - and we have two or three churches, and more chapels than I have yet added up. But public amusements are scarce with us. If a poor theatrical manager comes with his company to give us, in a loft, Mary Bax, or the Murder on the Sand Hills, we don't care much for him - starve him out, in fact. We take more kindly to wax-work, especially if it moves; in which case it keeps much clearer of the second commandment than when it is still. Cooke's Circus (Mr. Cooke is my friend, and always leaves a good name behind him) gives us only a night in passing through. Nor does the travelling menagerie think us worth a longer visit. It gave us a look-in the other day, bringing with it the residentiary van with the stained glass windows, which Her Majesty kept ready-made at Windsor Castle, until she found a suitable opportunity of submitting it for the proprietor's acceptance. I brought away five wonderments from this exhibition. I have wondered ever since, Whether the beasts ever do get used to those small places of confinement; Whether the monkeys have that very horrible flavour in their free state; Whether wild animals have a natural ear for time and tune, and therefore every four-footed creature began to howl in despair when the band began to play; What the giraffe does with his neck when his cart is shut up; and, Whether the elephant feels ashamed of himself when he is brought out of his den to stand on his head in the presence of the whole Collection.

We are a tidal harbour at Pavilionstone, as indeed I have implied already in my mention of tidal trains. At low water, we are a heap of mud, with an empty channel in it where a couple of men in big boots always shovel and scoop: with what exact object, I am unable to say. At that time, all the stranded fishing-boats turn over on their sides, as if they were dead marine monsters; the colliers and other shipping stick disconsolate in the mud; the steamers look as if their white chimneys would never smoke more, and their red paddles never turn again; the green sea-slime and weed upon the rough stones at the entrance, seem records of obsolete high tides never more to flow; the flagstaff-halyards droop; the very little wooden lighthouse shrinks in the idle glare of the sun. And here I may observe of the very little wooden lighthouse, that when it is lighted at night, - red and green, - it looks so like a medical man's, that several distracted husbands have at various times been found, on occasions of premature domestic anxiety, going round and round it, trying to find the Nightbell.

But, the moment the tide begins to make, the Pavilionstone Harbour begins to revive. It feels the breeze of the rising water before the water comes, and begins to flutter and stir. When the little shallow waves creep in, barely overlapping one another, the vanes at the mastheads wake, and become agitated. As the tide rises, the fishing-boats get into good spirits and dance, the flagstaff hoists a bright red flag, the steamboat smokes, cranes creak, horses and carriages dangle in the air, stray passengers and luggage appear. Now, the shipping is afloat, and comes up buoyantly, to look at the wharf. Now, the carts that have come down for coals, load away as hard as they can load. Now, the steamer smokes immensely, and occasionally blows at the paddle-boxes like a vaporous whale- greatly disturbing nervous loungers. Now, both the tide and the breeze have risen, and you are holding your hat on (if you want to see how the ladies hold THEIR hats on, with a stay, passing over the broad brim and down the nose, come to Pavilionstone). Now, everything in the harbour splashes, dashes, and bobs. Now, the Down Tidal Train is telegraphed, and you know (without knowing how you know), that two hundred and eighty-seven people are coming. Now, the fishing-boats that have been out, sail in at the top of the tide. Now, the bell goes, and the locomotive hisses and shrieks, and the train comes gliding in, and the two hundred and eighty-seven come scuffling out. Now, there is not only a tide of water, but a tide of people, and a tide of luggage - all tumbling and flowing and bouncing about together. Now, after infinite bustle, the steamer steams out, and we (on the Pier) are all delighted when she rolls as if she would roll her funnel out, and all are disappointed when she don't. Now, the other steamer is coming in, and the Custom House prepares, and the wharf-labourers assemble, and the hawsers are made ready, and the Hotel Porters come rattling down with van and truck, eager to begin more Olympic games with more luggage. And this is the way in which we go on, down at Pavilionstone, every tide. And, if you want to live a life of luggage, or to see it lived, or to breathe sweet air which will send you to sleep at a moment's notice at any period of the day or night, or to disport yourself upon or in the sea, or to scamper about Kent, or to come out of town for the enjoyment of all or any of these pleasures, come to Pavilionstone.

Down with the Tide

A very dark night it was, and bitter cold; the east wind blowing bleak, and bringing with it stinging particles from marsh, and moor, and fen - from the Great Desert and Old Egypt, may be. Some of the component parts of the sharp-edged vapour that came flying up the Thames at London might be mummy-dust, dry atoms from the Temple at Jerusalem, camels' foot-prints, crocodiles' hatching-places, loosened grains of expression from the visages of blunt- nosed sphinxes, waifs and strays from caravans of turbaned merchants, vegetation from jungles, frozen snow from the Himalayas. O! It was very, very dark upon the Thames, and it was bitter, bitter cold.

'And yet,' said the voice within the great pea-coat at my side, 'you'll have seen a good many rivers, too, I dare say?'

'Truly,' said I, 'when I come to think of it, not a few. From the Niagara, downward to the mountain rivers of Italy, which are like the national spirit - very tame, or chafing suddenly and bursting bounds, only to dwindle away again. The Moselle, and the Rhine, and the Rhone; and the Seine, and the Saone; and the St. Lawrence, Mississippi, and Ohio; and the Tiber, the Po, and the Arno; and the - '

Peacoat coughing as if he had had enough of that, I said no more. I could have carried the catalogue on to a teasing length, though, if I had been in the cruel mind.

'And after all,' said he, 'this looks so dismal?'

'So awful,' I returned, 'at night. The Seine at Paris is very gloomy too, at such a time, and is probably the scene of far more crime and greater wickedness; but this river looks so broad and vast, so murky and silent, seems such an image of death in the midst of the great city's life, that - '

That Peacoat coughed again. He COULD NOT stand my holding forth.

We were in a four-oared Thames Police Galley, lying on our oars in the deep shadow of Southwark Bridge - under the corner arch on the Surrey side - having come down with the tide from Vauxhall. We were fain to hold on pretty tight, though close in shore, for the river was swollen and the tide running down very strong. We were watching certain water-rats of human growth, and lay in the deep shade as quiet as mice; our light hidden and our scraps of conversation carried on in whispers. Above us, the massive iron girders of the arch were faintly visible, and below us its ponderous shadow seemed to sink down to the bottom of the stream.

We had been lying here some half an hour. With our backs to the wind, it is true; but the wind being in a determined temper blew straight through us, and would not take the trouble to go round. I would have boarded a fireship to get into action, and mildly suggested as much to my friend Pea.

'No doubt,' says he as patiently as possible; 'but shore-going tactics wouldn't do with us. River-thieves can always get rid of stolen property in a moment by dropping it overboard. We want to take them WITH the property, so we lurk about and come out upon 'em sharp. If they see us or hear us, over it goes.'

Pea's wisdom being indisputable, there was nothing for it but to sit there and be blown through, for another half-hour. The water- rats thinking it wise to abscond at the end of that time without commission of felony, we shot out, disappointed, with the tide.

'Grim they look, don't they?' said Pea, seeing me glance over my shoulder at the lights upon the bridge, and downward at their long crooked reflections in the river.

'Very,' said I, 'and make one think with a shudder of Suicides. What a night for a dreadful leap from that parapet!'

'Aye, but Waterloo's the favourite bridge for making holes in the water from,' returned Pea. 'By the bye - avast pulling, lads! - would you like to speak to Waterloo on the subject?'

My face confessing a surprised desire to have some friendly conversation with Waterloo Bridge, and my friend Pea being the most obliging of men, we put about, pulled out of the force of the stream, and in place of going at great speed with the tide, began to strive against it, close in shore again. Every colour but black seemed to have departed from the world. The air was black, the water was black, the barges and hulks were black, the piles were black, the buildings were black, the shadows were only a deeper shade of black upon a black ground. Here and there, a coal fire in an iron cresset blazed upon a wharf; but, one knew that it too had been black a little while ago, and would be black again soon. Uncomfortable rushes of water suggestive of gurgling and drowning, ghostly rattlings of iron chains, dismal clankings of discordant engines, formed the music that accompanied the dip of our oars and their rattling in the rowlocks. Even the noises had a black sound to me - as the trumpet sounded red to the blind man.

Our dexterous boat's crew made nothing of the tide, and pulled us gallantly up to Waterloo Bridge. Here Pea and I disembarked, passed under the black stone archway, and climbed the steep stone steps. Within a few feet of their summit, Pea presented me to Waterloo (or an eminent toll-taker representing that structure), muffled up to the eyes in a thick shawl, and amply great-coated and fur-capped.

Waterloo received us with cordiality, and observed of the night that it was 'a Searcher.' He had been originally called the Strand Bridge, he informed us, but had received his present name at the suggestion of the proprietors, when Parliament had resolved to vote three hundred thousand pound for the erection of a monument in honour of the victory. Parliament took the hint (said Waterloo, with the least flavour of misanthropy) and saved the money. Of course the late Duke of Wellington was the first passenger, and of course he paid his penny, and of course a noble lord preserved it evermore. The treadle and index at the toll-house (a most ingenious contrivance for rendering fraud impossible), were invented by Mr. Lethbridge, then property-man at Drury Lane Theatre.

Was it suicide, we wanted to know about? said Waterloo. Ha! Well, he had seen a good deal of that work, he did assure us. He had prevented some. Why, one day a woman, poorish looking, came in between the hatch, slapped down a penny, and wanted to go on without the change! Waterloo suspected this, and says to his mate, 'give an eye to the gate,' and bolted after her. She had got to the third seat between the piers, and was on the parapet just a going over, when he caught her and gave her in charge. At the police office next morning, she said it was along of trouble and a bad husband.

'Likely enough,' observed Waterloo to Pea and myself, as he adjusted his chin in his shawl. 'There's a deal of trouble about, you see - and bad husbands too!'

Another time, a young woman at twelve o'clock in the open day, got through, darted along; and, before Waterloo could come near her, jumped upon the parapet, and shot herself over sideways. Alarm given, watermen put off, lucky escape. - Clothes buoyed her up.

'This is where it is,' said Waterloo. 'If people jump off straight forwards from the middle of the parapet of the bays of the bridge, they are seldom killed by drowning, but are smashed, poor things; that's what THEY are; they dash themselves upon the buttress of the bridge. But you jump off,' said Waterloo to me, putting his fore-finger in a button-hole of my great-coat; 'you jump off from the side of the bay, and you'll tumble, true, into the stream under the arch. What you have got to do, is to mind how you jump in! There was poor Tom Steele from Dublin. Didn't dive! Bless you, didn't dive at all! Fell down so flat into the water, that he broke his breast-bone, and lived two days!'

I asked Waterloo if there were a favourite side of his bridge for this dreadful purpose? He reflected, and thought yes, there was. He should say the Surrey side.

Three decent-looking men went through one day, soberly and quietly, and went on abreast for about a dozen yards: when the middle one, he sung out, all of a sudden, 'Here goes, Jack!' and was over in a minute.

Body found? Well. Waterloo didn't rightly recollect about that. They were compositors, THEY were.

He considered it astonishing how quick people were! Why, there was a cab came up one Boxing-night, with a young woman in it, who looked, according to Waterloo's opinion of her, a little the worse for liquor; very handsome she was too - very handsome. She stopped the cab at the gate, and said she'd pay the cabman then, which she did, though there was a little hankering about the fare, because at first she didn't seem quite to know where she wanted to be drove to. However, she paid the man, and the toll too, and looking Waterloo in the face (he thought she knew him, don't you see!) said, 'I'll finish it somehow!' Well, the cab went off, leaving Waterloo a little doubtful in his mind, and while it was going on at full speed the young woman jumped out, never fell, hardly staggered, ran along the bridge pavement a little way, passing several people, and jumped over from the second opening. At the inquest it was giv' in evidence that she had been quarrelling at the Hero of Waterloo, and it was brought in jealousy. (One of the results of Waterloo's experience was, that there was a deal of jealousy about.)

'Do we ever get madmen?' said Waterloo, in answer to an inquiry of mine. 'Well, we DO get madmen. Yes, we have had one or two; escaped from 'Sylums, I suppose. One hadn't a halfpenny; and because I wouldn't let him through, he went back a little way, stooped down, took a run, and butted at the hatch like a ram. He smashed his hat rarely, but his head didn't seem no worse - in my opinion on account of his being wrong in it afore. Sometimes people haven't got a halfpenny. If they are really tired and poor we give 'em one and let 'em through. Other people will leave things - pocket-handkerchiefs mostly. I HAVE taken cravats and gloves, pocket-knives, tooth-picks, studs, shirt-pins, rings (generally from young gents, early in the morning), but handkerchiefs is the general thing.'

'Regular customers?' said Waterloo. 'Lord, yes! We have regular customers. One, such a worn-out, used-up old file as you can scarcely picter, comes from the Surrey side as regular as ten o'clock at night comes; and goes over, I think, to some flash house on the Middlesex side. He comes back, he does, as reg'lar as the clock strikes three in the morning, and then can hardly drag one of his old legs after the other. He always turns down the water- stairs, comes up again, and then goes on down the Waterloo Road. He always does the same thing, and never varies a minute. Does it every night - even Sundays.'

I asked Waterloo if he had given his mind to the possibility of this particular customer going down the water-stairs at three o'clock some morning, and never coming up again? He didn't think THAT of him, he replied. In fact, it was Waterloo's opinion, founded on his observation of that file, that he know'd a trick worth two of it.

'There's another queer old customer,' said Waterloo, 'comes over, as punctual as the almanack, at eleven o'clock on the sixth of January, at eleven o'clock on the fifth of April, at eleven o'clock on the sixth of July, at eleven o'clock on the tenth of October.

Drives a shaggy little, rough pony, in a sort of a rattle-trap arm- chair sort of a thing. White hair he has, and white whiskers, and muffles himself up with all manner of shawls. He comes back again the same afternoon, and we never see more of him for three months. He is a captain in the navy - retired - wery old - wery odd - and served with Lord Nelson. He is particular about drawing his pension at Somerset House afore the clock strikes twelve every quarter. I HAVE heerd say that he thinks it wouldn't be according to the Act of Parliament, if he didn't draw it afore twelve.'

Having related these anecdotes in a natural manner, which was the best warranty in the world for their genuine nature, our friend Waterloo was sinking deep into his shawl again, as having exhausted his communicative powers and taken in enough east wind, when my other friend Pea in a moment brought him to the surface by asking whether he had not been occasionally the subject of assault and battery in the execution of his duty? Waterloo recovering his spirits, instantly dashed into a new branch of his subject. We learnt how 'both these teeth' - here he pointed to the places where two front teeth were not - were knocked out by an ugly customer who one night made a dash at him (Waterloo) while his (the ugly customer's) pal and coadjutor made a dash at the toll-taking apron where the money-pockets were; how Waterloo, letting the teeth go (to Blazes, he observed indefinitely), grappled with the apron- seizer, permitting the ugly one to run away; and how he saved the bank, and captured his man, and consigned him to fine and imprisonment. Also how, on another night, 'a Cove' laid hold of Waterloo, then presiding at the horse-gate of his bridge, and threw him unceremoniously over his knee, having first cut his head open with his whip. How Waterloo 'got right,' and started after the Cove all down the Waterloo Road, through Stamford Street, and round to the foot of Blackfriars Bridge, where the Cove 'cut into' a public-house. How Waterloo cut in too; but how an aider and abettor of the Cove's, who happened to be taking a promiscuous drain at the bar, stopped Waterloo; and the Cove cut out again, ran across the road down Holland Street, and where not, and into a beer-shop. How Waterloo breaking away from his detainer was close upon the Cove's heels, attended by no end of people, who, seeing him running with the blood streaming down his face, thought something worse was 'up,' and roared Fire! and Murder! on the hopeful chance of the matter in hand being one or both. How the Cove was ignominiously taken, in a shed where he had run to hide, and how at the Police Court they at first wanted to make a sessions job of it; but eventually Waterloo was allowed to be 'spoke to,' and the Cove made it square with Waterloo by paying his doctor's bill (W. was laid up for a week) and giving him 'Three, ten.' Likewise we learnt what we had faintly suspected before, that your sporting amateur on the Derby day, albeit a captain, can be - 'if he be,' as Captain Bobadil observes, 'so generously minded' - anything but a man of honour and a gentleman; not sufficiently gratifying his nice sense of humour by the witty scattering of flour and rotten eggs on obtuse civilians, but requiring the further excitement of 'bilking the toll,' and 'Pitching into' Waterloo, and 'cutting him about the head with his whip;' finally being, when called upon to answer for the assault, what Waterloo described as 'Minus,' or, as I humbly conceived it, not to be found. Likewise did Waterloo inform us, in reply to my inquiries, admiringly and deferentially preferred through my friend Pea, that the takings at the Bridge had more than doubled in amount, since the reduction of the toll one half. And being asked if the aforesaid takings included much bad money, Waterloo responded, with a look far deeper than the deepest part of the river, HE should think not! - and so retired into his shawl for the rest of the night.

Then did Pea and I once more embark in our four-oared galley, and glide swiftly down the river with the tide. And while the shrewd East rasped and notched us, as with jagged razors, did my friend Pea impart to me confidences of interest relating to the Thames Police; we, between whiles, finding 'duty boats' hanging in dark corners under banks, like weeds - our own was a 'supervision boat' - and they, as they reported 'all right!' flashing their hidden light on us, and we flashing ours on them. These duty boats had one sitter in each: an Inspector: and were rowed 'Ran-dan,' which - for the information of those who never graduated, as I was once proud to do, under a fireman-waterman and winner of Kean's Prize Wherry: who, in the course of his tuition, took hundreds of gallons of rum and egg (at my expense) at the various houses of note above and below bridge; not by any means because he liked it, but to cure a weakness in his liver, for which the faculty had particularly recommended it - may be explained as rowed by three men, two pulling an oar each, and one a pair of sculls.

Thus, floating down our black highway, sullenly frowned upon by the knitted brows of Blackfriars, Southwark, and London, each in his lowering turn, I was shown by my friend Pea that there are, in the Thames Police Force, whose district extends from Battersea to Barking Creek, ninety-eight men, eight duty boats, and two supervision boats; and that these go about so silently, and lie in wait in such dark places, and so seem to be nowhere, and so may be anywhere, that they have gradually become a police of prevention, keeping the river almost clear of any great crimes, even while the increased vigilance on shore has made it much harder than of yore to live by 'thieving' in the streets. And as to the various kinds of water-thieves, said my friend Pea, there were the Tier-rangers, who silently dropped alongside the tiers of shipping in the Pool, by night, and who, going to the companion-head, listened for two snores - snore number one, the skipper's; snore number two, the mate's - mates and skippers always snoring great guns, and being dead sure to be hard at it if they had turned in and were asleep. Hearing the double fire, down went the Rangers into the skippers' cabins; groped for the skippers' inexpressibles, which it was the custom of those gentlemen to shake off, watch, money, braces, boots, and all together, on the floor; and therewith made off as silently as might be. Then there were the Lumpers, or labourers employed to unload vessels. They wore loose canvas jackets with a broad hem in the bottom, turned inside, so as to form a large circular pocket in which they could conceal, like clowns in pantomimes, packages of surprising sizes. A great deal of property was stolen in this manner (Pea confided to me) from steamers; first, because steamers carry a larger number of small packages than other ships; next, because of the extreme rapidity with which they are obliged to be unladen for their return voyages. The Lumpers dispose of their booty easily to marine store dealers, and the only remedy to be suggested is that marine store shops should be licensed, and thus brought under the eye of the police as rigidly as public-houses. Lumpers also smuggle goods ashore for the crews of vessels. The smuggling of tobacco is so considerable, that it is well worth the while of the sellers of smuggled tobacco to use hydraulic presses, to squeeze a single pound into a package small enough to be contained in an ordinary pocket. Next, said my friend Pea, there were the Truckers - less thieves than smugglers, whose business it was to land more considerable parcels of goods than the Lumpers could manage. They sometimes sold articles of grocery and so forth, to the crews, in order to cloak their real calling, and get aboard without suspicion. Many of them had boats of their own, and made money. Besides these, there were the Dredgermen, who, under pretence of dredging up coals and such like from the bottom of the river, hung about barges and other undecked craft, and when they saw an opportunity, threw any property they could lay their hands on overboard: in order slyly to dredge it up when the vessel was gone. Sometimes, they dexterously used their dredges to whip away anything that might lie within reach. Some of them were mighty neat at this, and the accomplishment was called dry dredging. Then, there was a vast deal of property, such as copper nails, sheathing, hardwood, &c., habitually brought away by shipwrights and other workmen from their employers' yards, and disposed of to marine store dealers, many of whom escaped detection through hard swearing, and their extraordinary artful ways of accounting for the possession of stolen property. Likewise, there were special-pleading practitioners, for whom barges 'drifted away of their own selves' - they having no hand in it, except first cutting them loose, and afterwards plundering them - innocents, meaning no harm, who had the misfortune to observe those foundlings wandering about the Thames.

We were now going in and out, with little noise and great nicety, among the tiers of shipping, whose many hulls, lying close together, rose out of the water like black streets. Here and there, a Scotch, an Irish, or a foreign steamer, getting up her steam as the tide made, looked, with her great chimney and high sides, like a quiet factory among the common buildings. Now, the streets opened into clearer spaces, now contracted into alleys; but the tiers were so like houses, in the dark, that I could almost have believed myself in the narrower bye-ways of Venice. Everything was wonderfully still; for, it wanted full three hours of flood, and nothing seemed awake but a dog here and there.

So we took no Tier-rangers captive, nor any Lumpers, nor Truckers, nor Dredgermen, nor other evil-disposed person or persons; but went ashore at Wapping, where the old Thames Police office is now a station-house, and where the old Court, with its cabin windows looking on the river, is a quaint charge room: with nothing worse in it usually than a stuffed cat in a glass case, and a portrait, pleasant to behold, of a rare old Thames Police officer, Mr. Superintendent Evans, now succeeded by his son. We looked over the charge books, admirably kept, and found the prevention so good that there were not five hundred entries (including drunken and disorderly) in a whole year. Then, we looked into the store-room; where there was an oakum smell, and a nautical seasoning of dreadnought clothing, rope yarn, boat-hooks, sculls and oars, spare stretchers, rudders, pistols, cutlasses, and the like. Then, into the cell, aired high up in the wooden wall through an opening like a kitchen plate-rack: wherein there was a drunken man, not at all warm, and very wishful to know if it were morning yet. Then, into a better sort of watch and ward room, where there was a squadron of stone bottles drawn up, ready to be filled with hot water and applied to any unfortunate creature who might be brought in apparently drowned. Finally, we shook hands with our worthy friend Pea, and ran all the way to Tower Hill, under strong Police suspicion occasionally, before we got warm.

The Long Voyage

When the wind is blowing and the sleet or rain is driving against the dark windows, I love to sit by the fire, thinking of what I have read in books of voyage and travel.

Such books have had a strong fascination for my mind from my earliest childhood; and I wonder it should have come to pass that I never have been round the world, never have been shipwrecked, ice-environed, tomahawked, or eaten.

Sitting on my ruddy hearth in the twilight of New Year's Eve, I find incidents of travel rise around me from all the latitudes and longitudes of the globe. They observe no order or sequence, but appear and vanish as they will - 'come like shadows, so depart.' Columbus, alone upon the sea with his disaffected crew, looks over the waste of waters from his high station on the poop of his ship, and sees the first uncertain glimmer of the light, 'rising and falling with the waves, like a torch in the bark of some fisherman,' which is the shining star of a new world. Bruce is caged in Abyssinia, surrounded by the gory horrors which shall often startle him out of his sleep at home when years have passed away. Franklin, come to the end of his unhappy overland journey - would that it had been his last! - lies perishing of hunger with his brave companions: each emaciated figure stretched upon its miserable bed without the power to rise: all, dividing the weary days between their prayers, their remembrances of the dear ones at home, and conversation on the pleasures of eating; the last-named topic being ever present to them, likewise, in their dreams. All the African travellers, wayworn, solitary and sad, submit themselves again to drunken, murderous, man-selling despots, of the lowest order of humanity; and Mungo Park, fainting under a tree and succoured by a woman, gratefully remembers how his Good Samaritan has always come to him in woman's shape, the wide world over.

A shadow on the wall in which my mind's eye can discern some traces of a rocky sea-coast, recalls to me a fearful story of travel derived from that unpromising narrator of such stories, a parliamentary blue-book. A convict is its chief figure, and this man escapes with other prisoners from a penal settlement. It is an island, and they seize a boat, and get to the main land. Their way is by a rugged and precipitous sea-shore, and they have no earthly hope of ultimate escape, for the party of soldiers despatched by an easier course to cut them off, must inevitably arrive at their distant bourne long before them, and retake them if by any hazard they survive the horrors of the way. Famine, as they all must have foreseen, besets them early in their course. Some of the party die and are eaten; some are murdered by the rest and eaten. This one awful creature eats his fill, and sustains his strength, and lives on to be recaptured and taken back. The unrelateable experiences through which he has passed have been so tremendous, that he is not hanged as he might be, but goes back to his old chained-gang work. A little time, and he tempts one other prisoner away, seizes another boat, and flies once more - necessarily in the old hopeless direction, for he can take no other. He is soon cut off, and met by the pursuing party face to face, upon the beach. He is alone. In his former journey he acquired an inappeasable relish for his dreadful food. He urged the new man away, expressly to kill him and eat him. In the pockets on one side of his coarse convict-dress, are portions of the man's body, on which he is regaling; in the pockets on the other side is an untouched store of salted pork (stolen before he left the island) for which he has no appetite. He is taken back, and he is hanged. But I shall never see that sea-beach on the wall or in the fire, without him, solitary monster, eating as he prowls along, while the sea rages and rises at him.

Captain Bligh (a worse man to be entrusted with arbitrary power there could scarcely be) is handed over the side of the Bounty, and turned adrift on the wide ocean in an open boat, by order of Fletcher Christian, one of his officers, at this very minute. Another flash of my fire, and 'Thursday October Christian,' five- and-twenty years of age, son of the dead and gone Fletcher by a savage mother, leaps aboard His Majesty's ship Briton, hove-to off Pitcairn's Island; says his simple grace before eating, in good English; and knows that a pretty little animal on board is called a dog, because in his childhood he had heard of such strange creatures from his father and the other mutineers, grown grey under the shade of the bread-fruit trees, speaking of their lost country far away.

See the Halsewell, East Indiaman outward bound, driving madly on a January night towards the rocks near Seacombe, on the island of Purbeck! The captain's two dear daughters are aboard, and five other ladies. The ship has been driving many hours, has seven feet water in her hold, and her mainmast has been cut away. The description of her loss, familiar to me from my early boyhood, seems to be read aloud as she rushes to her destiny.

'About two in the morning of Friday the sixth of January, the ship still driving, and approaching very fast to the shore, Mr. Henry Meriton, the second mate, went again into the cuddy, where the captain then was. Another conversation taking place, Captain Pierce expressed extreme anxiety for the preservation of his beloved daughters, and earnestly asked the officer if he could devise any method of saving them. On his answering with great concern, that he feared it would be impossible, but that their only chance would be to wait for morning, the captain lifted up his hands in silent and distressful ejaculation.

'At this dreadful moment, the ship struck, with such violence as to dash the heads of those standing in the cuddy against the deck above them, and the shock was accompanied by a shriek of horror that burst at one instant from every quarter of the ship.

'Many of the seamen, who had been remarkably inattentive and remiss in their duty during great part of the storm, now poured upon deck, where no exertions of the officers could keep them, while their assistance might have been useful. They had actually skulked in their hammocks, leaving the working of the pumps and other necessary labours to the officers of the ship, and the soldiers, who had made uncommon exertions. Roused by a sense of their danger, the same seamen, at this moment, in frantic exclamations, demanded of heaven and their fellow-sufferers that succour which their own efforts, timely made, might possibly have procured.

'The ship continued to beat on the rocks; and soon bilging, fell with her broadside towards the shore. When she struck, a number of the men climbed up the ensign-staff, under an apprehension of her immediately going to pieces.

'Mr. Meriton, at this crisis, offered to these unhappy beings the best advice which could be given; he recommended that all should come to the side of the ship lying lowest on the rocks, and singly to take the opportunities which might then offer, of escaping to the shore.

'Having thus provided, to the utmost of his power, for the safety of the desponding crew, he returned to the round-house, where, by this time, all the passengers and most of the officers had assembled. The latter were employed in offering consolation to the unfortunate ladies; and, with unparalleled magnanimity, suffering their compassion for the fair and amiable companions of their misfortunes to prevail over the sense of their own danger.

'In this charitable work of comfort, Mr. Meriton now joined, by assurances of his opinion, that, the ship would hold together till the morning, when all would be safe. Captain Pierce, observing one of the young gentlemen loud in his exclamations of terror, and frequently cry that the ship was parting, cheerfully bid him be quiet, remarking that though the ship should go to pieces, he would not, but would be safe enough.

'It is difficult to convey a correct idea of the scene of this deplorable catastrophe, without describing the place where it happened. The Haleswell struck on the rocks at a part of the shore where the cliff is of vast height, and rises almost perpendicular from its base. But at this particular spot, the foot of the cliff is excavated into a cavern of ten or twelve yards in depth, and of breadth equal to the length of a large ship. The sides of the cavern are so nearly upright, as to be of extremely difficult access; and the bottom is strewed with sharp and uneven rocks, which seem, by some convulsion of the earth, to have been detached from its roof.

'The ship lay with her broadside opposite to the mouth of this cavern, with her whole length stretched almost from side to side of it. But when she struck, it was too dark for the unfortunate persons on board to discover the real magnitude of the danger, and the extreme horror of such a situation.

'In addition to the company already in the round-house, they had admitted three black women and two soldiers' wives; who, with the husband of one of them, had been allowed to come in, though the seamen, who had tumultuously demanded entrance to get the lights, had been opposed and kept out by Mr. Rogers and Mr. Brimer, the third and fifth mates. The numbers there were, therefore, now increased to near fifty. Captain Pierce sat on a chair, a cot, or some other moveable, with a daughter on each side, whom he alternately pressed to his affectionate breast. The rest of the melancholy assembly were seated on the deck, which was strewed with musical instruments, and the wreck of furniture and other articles.

'Here also Mr. Meriton, after having cut several wax-candles in pieces, and stuck them up in various parts of the round-house, and lighted up all the glass lanthorns he could find, took his seat, intending to wait the approach of dawn; and then assist the partners of his dangers to escape. But, observing that the poor ladies appeared parched and exhausted, he brought a basket of oranges and prevailed on some of them to refresh themselves by sucking a little of the juice. At this time they were all tolerably composed, except Miss Mansel, who was in hysteric fits on the floor of the deck of the round-house.

'But on Mr. Meriton's return to the company, he perceived a considerable alteration in the appearance of the ship; the sides were visibly giving way; the deck seemed to be lifting, and he discovered other strong indications that she could not hold much longer together. On this account, he attempted to go forward to look out, but immediately saw that the ship had separated in the middle, and that the forepart having changed its position, lay rather further out towards the sea. In such an emergency, when the next moment might plunge him into eternity, he determined to seize the present opportunity, and follow the example of the crew and the soldiers, who were now quitting the ship in numbers, and making their way to the shore, though quite ignorant of its nature and description.

'Among other expedients, the ensign-staff had been unshipped, and attempted to be laid between the ship's side and some of the rocks, but without success, for it snapped asunder before it reached them. However, by the light of a lanthorn, which a seaman handed through the skylight of the round-house to the deck, Mr. Meriton discovered a spar which appeared to be laid from the ship's side to the rocks, and on this spar he resolved to attempt his escape.

'Accordingly, lying down upon it, he thrust himself forward; however, he soon found that it had no communication with the rock; he reached the end of it, and then slipped off, receiving a very violent bruise in his fall, and before he could recover his legs, he was washed off by the surge. He now supported himself by swimming, until a returning wave dashed him against the back part of the cavern. Here he laid hold of a small projection in the rock, but was so much benumbed that he was on the point of quitting it, when a seaman, who had already gained a footing, extended his hand, and assisted him until he could secure himself a little on the rock; from which he clambered on a shelf still higher, and out of the reach of the surf.

'Mr. Rogers, the third mate, remained with the captain and the unfortunate ladies and their companions nearly twenty minutes after Mr. Meriton had quitted the ship. Soon after the latter left the round-house, the captain asked what was become of him, to which Mr. Rogers replied, that he was gone on deck to see what could be done. After this, a heavy sea breaking over the ship, the ladies exclaimed, "Oh, poor Meriton! he is drowned; had he stayed with us he would have been safe!" and they all, particularly Miss Mary Pierce, expressed great concern at the apprehension of his loss.

'The sea was now breaking in at the fore part of the ship, and reached as far as the mainmast. Captain Pierce gave Mr. Rogers a nod, and they took a lamp and went together into the stern-gallery, where, after viewing the rocks for some time, Captain Pierce asked Mr. Rogers if he thought there was any possibility of saving the girls; to which he replied, he feared there was none; for they could only discover the black face of the perpendicular rock, and not the cavern which afforded shelter to those who escaped. They then returned to the round-house, where Mr. Rogers hung up the lamp, and Captain Pierce sat down between his two daughters.

'The sea continuing to break in very fast, Mr. Macmanus, a midshipman, and Mr. Schutz, a passenger, asked Mr. Rogers what they could do to escape. "Follow me," he replied, and they all went into the stern-gallery, and from thence to the upper-quarter- gallery on the poop. While there, a very heavy sea fell on board, and the round-house gave way; Mr. Rogers heard the ladies shriek at intervals, as if the water reached them; the noise of the sea at other times drowning their voices.

'Mr. Brimer had followed him to the poop, where they remained together about five minutes, when on the breaking of this heavy sea, they jointly seized a hen-coop. The same wave which proved fatal to some of those below, carried him and his companion to the rock, on which they were violently dashed and miserably bruised.

'Here on the rock were twenty-seven men; but it now being low water, and as they were convinced that on the flowing of the tide all must be washed off, many attempted to get to the back or the sides of the cavern, beyond the reach of the returning sea. Scarcely more than six, besides Mr. Rogers and Mr. Brimer, succeeded.

'Mr. Rogers, on gaining this station, was so nearly exhausted, that had his exertions been protracted only a few minutes longer, he must have sunk under them. He was now prevented from joining Mr. Meriton, by at least twenty men between them, none of whom could move, without the imminent peril of his life.

'They found that a very considerable number of the crew, seamen and soldiers, and some petty officers, were in the same situation as themselves, though many who had reached the rocks below, perished in attempting to ascend. They could yet discern some part of the ship, and in their dreary station solaced themselves with the hopes of its remaining entire until day-break; for, in the midst of their own distress, the sufferings of the females on board affected them with the most poignant anguish; and every sea that broke inspired them with terror for their safety.

'But, alas, their apprehensions were too soon realised! Within a very few minutes of the time that Mr. Rogers gained the rock, an universal shriek, which long vibrated in their ears, in which the voice of female distress was lamentably distinguished, announced the dreadful catastrophe. In a few moments all was hushed, except the roaring of the winds and the dashing of the waves; the wreck was buried in the deep, and not an atom of it was ever afterwards seen.'

The most beautiful and affecting incident I know, associated with a shipwreck, succeeds this dismal story for a winter night. The Grosvenor, East Indiaman, homeward bound, goes ashore on the coast of Caffraria. It is resolved that the officers, passengers, and crew, in number one hundred and thirty-five souls, shall endeavour to penetrate on foot, across trackless deserts, infested by wild beasts and cruel savages, to the Dutch settlements at the Cape of Good Hope. With this forlorn object before them, they finally separate into two parties - never more to meet on earth.

There is a solitary child among the passengers - a little boy of seven years old who has no relation there; and when the first party is moving away he cries after some member of it who has been kind to him. The crying of a child might be supposed to be a little thing to men in such great extremity; but it touches them, and he is immediately taken into that detachment.

From which time forth, this child is sublimely made a sacred charge. He is pushed, on a little raft, across broad rivers by the swimming sailors; they carry him by turns through the deep sand and long grass (he patiently walking at all other times); they share with him such putrid fish as they find to eat; they lie down and wait for him when the rough carpenter, who becomes his especial friend, lags behind. Beset by lions and tigers, by savages, by thirst, by hunger, by death in a crowd of ghastly shapes, they never - O Father of all mankind, thy name be blessed for it! - forget this child. The captain stops exhausted, and his faithful coxswain goes back and is seen to sit down by his side, and neither of the two shall be any more beheld until the great last day; but, as the rest go on for their lives, they take the child with them. The carpenter dies of poisonous berries eaten in starvation; and the steward, succeeding to the command of the party, succeeds to the sacred guardianship of the child.

God knows all he does for the poor baby; how he cheerfully carries him in his arms when he himself is weak and ill; how he feeds him when he himself is griped with want; how he folds his ragged jacket round him, lays his little worn face with a woman's tenderness upon his sunburnt breast, soothes him in his sufferings, sings to him as he limps along, unmindful of his own parched and bleeding feet. Divided for a few days from the rest, they dig a grave in the sand and bury their good friend the cooper - these two companions alone in the wilderness - and then the time comes when they both are ill, and beg their wretched partners in despair, reduced and few in number now, to wait by them one day. They wait by them one day, they wait by them two days. On the morning of the third, they move very softly about, in making their preparations for the resumption of their journey; for, the child is sleeping by the fire, and it is agreed with one consent that he shall not be disturbed until the last moment. The moment comes, the fire is dying - and the child is dead.

His faithful friend, the steward, lingers but a little while behind him. His grief is great, he staggers on for a few days, lies down in the desert, and dies. But he shall be re-united in his immortal spirit - who can doubt it! - with the child, when he and the poor carpenter shall be raised up with the words, 'Inasmuch as ye have done it unto the least of these, ye have done it unto Me.'

As I recall the dispersal and disappearance of nearly all the participators in this once famous shipwreck (a mere handful being recovered at last), and the legends that were long afterwards revived from time to time among the English officers at the Cape, of a white woman with an infant, said to have been seen weeping outside a savage hut far in the interior, who was whisperingly associated with the remembrance of the missing ladies saved from the wrecked vessel, and who was often sought but never found, thoughts of another kind of travel came into my mind.

Thoughts of a voyager unexpectedly summoned from home, who travelled a vast distance, and could never return. Thoughts of this unhappy wayfarer in the depths of his sorrow, in the bitterness of his anguish, in the helplessness of his self-reproach, in the desperation of his desire to set right what he had left wrong, and do what he had left undone.

For, there were many, many things he had neglected. Little matters while he was at home and surrounded by them, but things of mighty moment when he was at an immeasurable distance. There were many many blessings that he had inadequately felt, there were many trivial injuries that he had not forgiven, there was love that he had but poorly returned, there was friendship that he had too lightly prized: there were a million kind words that he might have spoken, a million kind looks that he might have given, uncountable slight easy deeds in which he might have been most truly great and good. O for a day (he would exclaim), for but one day to make amends! But the sun never shone upon that happy day, and out of his remote captivity he never came.

Why does this traveller's fate obscure, on New Year's Eve, the other histories of travellers with which my mind was filled but now, and cast a solemn shadow over me! Must I one day make his journey? Even so. Who shall say, that I may not then be tortured by such late regrets: that I may not then look from my exile on my empty place and undone work? I stand upon a sea-shore, where the waves are years. They break and fall, and I may little heed them; but, with every wave the sea is rising, and I know that it will float me on this traveller's voyage at last.

A Monument of French Folly

It was profoundly observed by a witty member of the Court of Common Council, in Council assembled in the City of London, in the year of our Lord one thousand eight hundred and fifty, that the French are a frog-eating people, who wear wooden shoes.

We are credibly informed, in reference to the nation whom this choice spirit so happily disposed of, that the caricatures and stage representations which were current in England some half a century ago, exactly depict their present condition. For example, we understand that every Frenchman, without exception, wears a pigtail and curl-papers. That he is extremely sallow, thin, long- faced, and lantern-jawed. That the calves of his legs are invariably undeveloped; that his legs fail at the knees, and that his shoulders are always higher than his ears. We are likewise assured that he rarely tastes any food but soup maigre, and an onion; that he always says, 'By Gar! Aha! Vat you tell me, sare?' at the end of every sentence he utters; and that the true generic name of his race is the Mounseers, or the Parly-voos. If he be not a dancing-master, or a barber, he must be a cook; since no other trades but those three are congenial to the tastes of the people, or permitted by the Institutions of the country. He is a slave, of course. The ladies of France (who are also slaves) invariably have their heads tied up in Belcher handkerchiefs, wear long earrings, carry tambourines, and beguile the weariness of their yoke by singing in head voices through their noses - principally to barrel- organs.

It may be generally summed up, of this inferior people, that they have no idea of anything.

Of a great Institution like Smithfield, they are unable to form the least conception. A Beast Market in the heart of Paris would be regarded an impossible nuisance. Nor have they any notion of slaughter-houses in the midst of a city. One of these benighted frog-eaters would scarcely understand your meaning, if you told him of the existence of such a British bulwark.

It is agreeable, and perhaps pardonable, to indulge in a little self-complacency when our right to it is thoroughly established. At the present time, to be rendered memorable by a final attack on that good old market which is the (rotten) apple of the Corporation's eye, let us compare ourselves, to our national delight and pride as to these two subjects of slaughter-house and beast-market, with the outlandish foreigner.

The blessings of Smithfield are too well understood to need recapitulation; all who run (away from mad bulls and pursuing oxen) may read. Any market-day they may be beheld in glorious action. Possibly the merits of our slaughter-houses are not yet quite so generally appreciated.

Slaughter-houses, in the large towns of England, are always (with the exception of one or two enterprising towns) most numerous in the most densely crowded places, where there is the least circulation of air. They are often underground, in cellars; they are sometimes in close back yards; sometimes (as in Spitalfields) in the very shops where the meat is sold. Occasionally, under good private management, they are ventilated and clean. For the most part, they are unventilated and dirty; and, to the reeking walls, putrid fat and other offensive animal matter clings with a tenacious hold. The busiest slaughter-houses in London are in the neighbourhood of Smithfield, in Newgate Market, in Whitechapel, in Newport Market, in Leadenhall Market, in Clare Market. All these places are surrounded by houses of a poor description, swarming with inhabitants. Some of them are close to the worst burial-grounds in London. When the slaughter-house is below the ground, it is a common practice to throw the sheep down areas, neck and crop - which is exciting, but not at all cruel. When it is on the level surface, it is often extremely difficult of approach. Then, the beasts have to be worried, and goaded, and pronged, and tail- twisted, for a long time before they can be got in - which is entirely owing to their natural obstinacy. When it is not difficult of approach, but is in a foul condition, what they see and scent makes them still more reluctant to enter - which is their natural obstinacy again. When they do get in at last, after no trouble and suffering to speak of (for, there is nothing in the previous journey into the heart of London, the night's endurance in Smithfield, the struggle out again, among the crowded multitude, the coaches, carts, waggons, omnibuses, gigs, chaises, phaetons, cabs, trucks, dogs, boys, whoopings, roarings, and ten thousand other distractions), they are represented to be in a most unfit state to be killed, according to microscopic examinations made of their fevered blood by one of the most distinguished physiologists in the world, PROFESSOR OWEN - but that's humbug. When they ARE killed, at last, their reeking carcases are hung in impure air, to become, as the same Professor will explain to you, less nutritious and more unwholesome - but he is only an UNcommon counsellor, so don't mind HIM. In half a quarter of a mile's length of Whitechapel, at one time, there shall be six hundred newly slaughtered oxen hanging up, and seven hundred sheep - but, the more the merrier - proof of prosperity. Hard by Snow Hill and Warwick Lane, you shall see the little children, inured to sights of brutality from their birth, trotting along the alleys, mingled with troops of horribly busy pigs, up to their ankles in blood - but it makes the young rascals hardy. Into the imperfect sewers of this overgrown city, you shall have the immense mass of corruption, engendered by these practices, lazily thrown out of sight, to rise, in poisonous gases, into your house at night, when your sleeping children will most readily absorb them, and to find its languid way, at last, into the river that you drink - but, the French are a frog-eating people who wear wooden shoes, and it's O the roast beef of England, my boy, the jolly old English roast beef.

It is quite a mistake - a newfangled notion altogether - to suppose that there is any natural antagonism between putrefaction and health. They know better than that, in the Common Council. You may talk about Nature, in her wisdom, always warning man through his sense of smell, when he draws near to something dangerous; but, that won't go down in the City. Nature very often don't mean anything. Mrs. Quickly says that prunes are ill for a green wound; but whosoever says that putrid animal substances are ill for a green wound, or for robust vigour, or for anything or for anybody, is a humanity-monger and a humbug. Britons never, never, never, &c., therefore. And prosperity to cattle-driving, cattle- slaughtering, bone-crushing, blood-boiling, trotter-scraping, tripe-dressing, paunch-cleaning, gut-spinning, hide-preparing, tallow-melting, and other salubrious proceedings, in the midst of hospitals, churchyards, workhouses, schools, infirmaries, refuges, dwellings, provision-shops nurseries, sick-beds, every stage and baiting-place in the journey from birth to death!

These UNcommon counsellors, your Professor Owens and fellows, will contend that to tolerate these things in a civilised city, is to reduce it to a worse condition than BRUCE found to prevail in ABYSSINIA. For there (say they) the jackals and wild dogs came at night to devour the offal; whereas, here there are no such natural scavengers, and quite as savage customs. Further, they will demonstrate that nothing in Nature is intended to be wasted, and that besides the waste which such abuses occasion in the articles of health and life - main sources of the riches of any community - they lead to a prodigious waste of changing matters, which might, with proper preparation, and under scientific direction, be safely applied to the increase of the fertility of the land. Thus (they argue) does Nature ever avenge infractions of her beneficent laws, and so surely as Man is determined to warp any of her blessings into curses, shall they become curses, and shall he suffer heavily. But, this is cant. Just as it is cant of the worst description to say to the London Corporation, 'How can you exhibit to the people so plain a spectacle of dishonest equivocation, as to claim the right of holding a market in the midst of the great city, for one of your vested privileges, when you know that when your last market holding charter was granted to you by King Charles the First, Smithfield stood IN THE SUBURBS OF LONDON, and is in that very charter so described in those five words?' - which is certainly true, but has nothing to do with the question.

Now to the comparison, in these particulars of civilisation, between the capital of England, and the capital of that frog-eating and wooden-shoe wearing country, which the illustrious Common Councilman so sarcastically settled.

In Paris, there is no Cattle Market. Cows and calves are sold within the city, but, the Cattle Markets are at Poissy, about thirteen miles off, on a line of railway; and at Sceaux, about five miles off. The Poissy market is held every Thursday; the Sceaux market, every Monday. In Paris, there are no slaughter-houses, in our acceptation of the term. There are five public Abattoirs - within the walls, though in the suburbs - and in these all the slaughtering for the city must be performed. They are managed by a Syndicat or Guild of Butchers, who confer with the Minister of the Interior on all matters affecting the trade, and who are consulted when any new regulations are contemplated for its government. They are, likewise, under the vigilant superintendence of the police. Every butcher must be licensed: which proves him at once to be a slave, for we don't license butchers in England - we only license apothecaries, attorneys, post-masters, publicans, hawkers, retailers of tobacco, snuff, pepper, and vinegar - and one or two other little trades, not worth mentioning. Every arrangement in connexion with the slaughtering and sale of meat, is matter of strict police regulation. (Slavery again, though we certainly have a general sort of Police Act here.)

But, in order that the reader may understand what a monument of folly these frog-eaters have raised in their abattoirs and cattle- markets, and may compare it with what common counselling has done for us all these years, and would still do but for the innovating spirit of the times, here follows a short account of a recent visit to these places:

It was as sharp a February morning as you would desire to feel at your fingers' ends when I turned out - tumbling over a chiffonier with his little basket and rake, who was picking up the bits of coloured paper that had been swept out, over-night, from a Bon-Bon shop - to take the Butchers' Train to Poissy. A cold, dim light just touched the high roofs of the Tuileries which have seen such changes, such distracted crowds, such riot and bloodshed; and they looked as calm, and as old, all covered with white frost, as the very Pyramids. There was not light enough, yet, to strike upon the towers of Notre Dame across the water; but I thought of the dark pavement of the old Cathedral as just beginning to be streaked with grey; and of the lamps in the 'House of God,' the Hospital close to it, burning low and being quenched; and of the keeper of the Morgue going about with a fading lantern, busy in the arrangement of his terrible waxwork for another sunny day.

The sun was up, and shining merrily when the butchers and I, announcing our departure with an engine shriek to sleepy Paris, rattled away for the Cattle Market. Across the country, over the Seine, among a forest of scrubby trees - the hoar frost lying cold in shady places, and glittering in the light - and here we are - at Poissy! Out leap the butchers, who have been chattering all the way like madmen, and off they straggle for the Cattle Market (still chattering, of course, incessantly), in hats and caps of all shapes, in coats and blouses, in calf-skins, cow-skins, horse- skins, furs, shaggy mantles, hairy coats, sacking, baize, oil-skin, anything you please that will keep a man and a butcher warm, upon a frosty morning.

Many a French town have I seen, between this spot of ground and Strasburg or Marseilles, that might sit for your picture, little Poissy! Barring the details of your old church, I know you well, albeit we make acquaintance, now, for the first time. I know your narrow, straggling, winding streets, with a kennel in the midst, and lamps slung across. I know your picturesque street-corners, winding up-hill Heaven knows why or where! I know your tradesmen's inscriptions, in letters not quite fat enough; your barbers' brazen basins dangling over little shops; your Cafes and Estaminets, with cloudy bottles of stale syrup in the windows, and pictures of crossed billiard cues outside. I know this identical grey horse with his tail rolled up in a knot like the 'back hair' of an untidy woman, who won't be shod, and who makes himself heraldic by clattering across the street on his hind-legs, while twenty voices shriek and growl at him as a Brigand, an accursed Robber, and an everlastingly-doomed Pig. I know your sparkling town-fountain, too, my Poissy, and am glad to see it near a cattle-market, gushing so freshly, under the auspices of a gallant little sublimated Frenchman wrought in metal, perched upon the top. Through all the land of France I know this unswept room at The Glory, with its peculiar smell of beans and coffee, where the butchers crowd about the stove, drinking the thinnest of wine from the smallest of tumblers; where the thickest of coffee-cups mingle with the longest of loaves, and the weakest of lump sugar; where Madame at the counter easily acknowledges the homage of all entering and departing butchers; where the billiard-table is covered up in the midst like a great bird-cake - but the bird may sing by-and-by!

A bell! The Calf Market! Polite departure of butchers. Hasty payment and departure on the part of amateur Visitor. Madame reproaches Ma'amselle for too fine a susceptibility in reference to the devotion of a Butcher in a bear-skin. Monsieur, the landlord of The Glory, counts a double handful of sous, without an unobliterated inscription, or an undamaged crowned head, among them.

There is little noise without, abundant space, and no confusion. The open area devoted to the market is divided into three portions: the Calf Market, the Cattle Market, the Sheep Market. Calves at eight, cattle at ten, sheep at mid-day. All is very clean.

The Calf Market is a raised platform of stone, some three or four feet high, open on all sides, with a lofty overspreading roof, supported on stone columns, which give it the appearance of a sort of vineyard from Northern Italy. Here, on the raised pavement, lie innumerable calves, all bound hind-legs and fore-legs together, and all trembling violently - perhaps with cold, perhaps with fear, perhaps with pain; for, this mode of tying, which seems to be an absolute superstition with the peasantry, can hardly fail to cause great suffering. Here, they lie, patiently in rows, among the straw, with their stolid faces and inexpressive eyes, superintended by men and women, boys and girls; here they are inspected by our friends, the butchers, bargained for, and bought. Plenty of time; plenty of room; plenty of good humour. 'Monsieur Francois in the bear-skin, how do you do, my friend? You come from Paris by the train? The fresh air does you good. If you are in want of three or four fine calves this market morning, my angel, I, Madame Doche, shall be happy to deal with you. Behold these calves, Monsieur Francois! Great Heaven, you are doubtful! Well, sir, walk round and look about you. If you find better for the money, buy them. If not, come to me!' Monsieur Francois goes his way leisurely, and keeps a wary eye upon the stock. No other butcher jostles Monsieur Francois; Monsieur Francois jostles no other butcher. Nobody is flustered and aggravated. Nobody is savage. In the midst of the country blue frocks and red handkerchiefs, and the butchers' coats, shaggy, furry, and hairy: of calf-skin, cow-skin, horse-skin, and bear-skin: towers a cocked hat and a blue cloak. Slavery! For OUR Police wear great-coats and glazed hats.

But now the bartering is over, and the calves are sold. 'Ho! Gregoire, Antoine, Jean, Louis! Bring up the carts, my children! Quick, brave infants! Hola! Hi!'

The carts, well littered with straw, are backed up to the edge of the raised pavement, and various hot infants carry calves upon their heads, and dexterously pitch them in, while other hot infants, standing in the carts, arrange the calves, and pack them carefully in straw. Here is a promising young calf, not sold, whom Madame Doche unbinds. Pardon me, Madame Doche, but I fear this mode of tying the four legs of a quadruped together, though strictly a la mode, is not quite right. You observe, Madame Doche, that the cord leaves deep indentations in the skin, and that the animal is so cramped at first as not to know, or even remotely suspect that HE is unbound, until you are so obliging as to kick him, in your delicate little way, and pull his tail like a bell- rope. Then, he staggers to his knees, not being able to stand, and stumbles about like a drunken calf, or the horse at Franconi's, whom you may have seen, Madame Doche, who is supposed to have been mortally wounded in battle. But, what is this rubbing against me, as I apostrophise Madame Doche? It is another heated infant with a calf upon his head. 'Pardon, Monsieur, but will you have the politeness to allow me to pass?' 'Ah, sir, willingly. I am vexed to obstruct the way.' On he staggers, calf and all, and makes no allusion whatever either to my eyes or limbs.

Now, the carts are all full. More straw, my Antoine, to shake over these top rows; then, off we will clatter, rumble, jolt, and rattle, a long row of us, out of the first town-gate, and out at the second town-gate, and past the empty sentry-box, and the little thin square bandbox of a guardhouse, where nobody seems to live: and away for Paris, by the paved road, lying, a straight, straight line, in the long, long avenue of trees. We can neither choose our road, nor our pace, for that is all prescribed to us. The public convenience demands that our carts should get to Paris by such a route, and no other (Napoleon had leisure to find that out, while he had a little war with the world upon his hands), and woe betide us if we infringe orders.

Drovers of oxen stand in the Cattle Market, tied to iron bars fixed into posts of granite. Other droves advance slowly down the long avenue, past the second town-gate, and the first town-gate, and the sentry-box, and the bandbox, thawing the morning with their smoky breath as they come along. Plenty of room; plenty of time. Neither man nor beast is driven out of his wits by coaches, carts, waggons, omnibuses, gigs, chaises, phaetons, cabs, trucks, boys, whoopings, roarings, and multitudes. No tail-twisting is necessary - no iron pronging is necessary. There are no iron prongs here. The market for cattle is held as quietly as the market for calves. In due time, off the cattle go to Paris; the drovers can no more choose their road, nor their time, nor the numbers they shall drive, than they can choose their hour for dying in the course of nature.

Sheep next. The sheep-pens are up here, past the Branch Bank of Paris established for the convenience of the butchers, and behind the two pretty fountains they are making in the Market. My name is Bull: yet I think I should like to see as good twin fountains - not to say in Smithfield, but in England anywhere. Plenty of room; plenty of time. And here are sheep-dogs, sensible as ever, but with a certain French air about them - not without a suspicion of dominoes - with a kind of flavour of moustache and beard - demonstrative dogs, shaggy and loose where an English dog would be tight and close - not so troubled with business calculations as our English drovers' dogs, who have always got their sheep upon their minds, and think about their work, even resting, as you may see by their faces; but, dashing, showy, rather unreliable dogs: who might worry me instead of their legitimate charges if they saw occasion - and might see it somewhat suddenly.

The market for sheep passes off like the other two; and away they go, by THEIR allotted road to Paris. My way being the Railway, I make the best of it at twenty miles an hour; whirling through the now high-lighted landscape; thinking that the inexperienced green buds will be wishing, before long, they had not been tempted to come out so soon; and wondering who lives in this or that chateau, all window and lattice, and what the family may have for breakfast this sharp morning.

After the Market comes the Abattoir. What abattoir shall I visit first? Montmartre is the largest. So I will go there.

The abattoirs are all within the walls of Paris, with an eye to the receipt of the octroi duty; but, they stand in open places in the suburbs, removed from the press and bustle of the city. They are managed by the Syndicat or Guild of Butchers, under the inspection of the Police. Certain smaller items of the revenue derived from them are in part retained by the Guild for the payment of their expenses, and in part devoted by it to charitable purposes in connexion with the trade. They cost six hundred and eighty thousand pounds; and they return to the city of Paris an interest on that outlay, amounting to nearly six and a-half per cent.

Here, in a sufficiently dismantled space is the Abattoir of Montmartre, covering nearly nine acres of ground, surrounded by a high wall, and looking from the outside like a cavalry barrack. At the iron gates is a small functionary in a large cocked hat. 'Monsieur desires to see the abattoir? Most certainly.' State being inconvenient in private transactions, and Monsieur being already aware of the cocked hat, the functionary puts it into a little official bureau which it almost fills, and accompanies me in the modest attire - as to his head - of ordinary life.

Many of the animals from Poissy have come here. On the arrival of each drove, it was turned into yonder ample space, where each butcher who had bought, selected his own purchases. Some, we see now, in these long perspectives of stalls with a high over-hanging roof of wood and open tiles rising above the walls. While they rest here, before being slaughtered, they are required to be fed and watered, and the stalls must be kept clean. A stated amount of fodder must always be ready in the loft above; and the supervision is of the strictest kind. The same regulations apply to sheep and calves; for which, portions of these perspectives are strongly railed off. All the buildings are of the strongest and most solid description.

After traversing these lairs, through which, besides the upper provision for ventilation just mentioned, there may be a thorough current of air from opposite windows in the side walls, and from doors at either end, we traverse the broad, paved, court-yard until we come to the slaughter-houses. They are all exactly alike, and adjoin each other, to the number of eight or nine together, in blocks of solid building. Let us walk into the first.

It is firmly built and paved with stone. It is well lighted, thoroughly aired, and lavishly provided with fresh water. It has two doors opposite each other; the first, the door by which I entered from the main yard; the second, which is opposite, opening on another smaller yard, where the sheep and calves are killed on benches. The pavement of that yard, I see, slopes downward to a gutter, for its being more easily cleansed. The slaughter-house is fifteen feet high, sixteen feet and a-half wide, and thirty-three feet long. It is fitted with a powerful windlass, by which one man at the handle can bring the head of an ox down to the ground to receive the blow from the pole-axe that is to fell him - with the means of raising the carcass and keeping it suspended during the after-operation of dressing - and with hooks on which carcasses can hang, when completely prepared, without touching the walls. Upon the pavement of this first stone chamber, lies an ox scarcely dead. If I except the blood draining from him, into a little stone well in a corner of the pavement, the place is free from offence as the Place de la Concorde. It is infinitely purer and cleaner, I know, my friend the functionary, than the Cathedral of Notre Dame. Ha, ha! Monsieur is pleasant, but, truly, there is reason, too, in what he says.

I look into another of these slaughter-houses. 'Pray enter,' says a gentleman in bloody boots. 'This is a calf I have killed this morning. Having a little time upon my hands, I have cut and punctured this lace pattern in the coats of his stomach. It is pretty enough. I did it to divert myself.' - 'It is beautiful, Monsieur, the slaughterer!' He tells me I have the gentility to say so.

I look into rows of slaughter-houses. In many, retail dealers, who have come here for the purpose, are making bargains for meat. There is killing enough, certainly, to satiate an unused eye; and there are steaming carcasses enough, to suggest the expediency of a fowl and salad for dinner; but, everywhere, there is an orderly, clean, well-systematised routine of work in progress - horrible work at the best, if you please; but, so much the greater reason why it should be made the best of. I don't know (I think I have observed, my name is Bull) that a Parisian of the lowest order is particularly delicate, or that his nature is remarkable for an infinitesimal infusion of ferocity; but, I do know, my potent, grave, and common counselling Signors, that he is forced, when at this work, to submit himself to a thoroughly good system, and to make an Englishman very heartily ashamed of you.

Here, within the walls of the same abattoir, in other roomy and commodious buildings, are a place for converting the fat into tallow and packing it for market - a place for cleansing and scalding calves' heads and sheep's feet - a place for preparing tripe - stables and coach-houses for the butchers - innumerable conveniences, aiding in the diminution of offensiveness to its lowest possible point, and the raising of cleanliness and supervision to their highest. Hence, all the meat that goes out of the gate is sent away in clean covered carts. And if every trade connected with the slaughtering of animals were obliged by law to be carried on in the same place, I doubt, my friend, now reinstated in the cocked hat (whose civility these two francs imperfectly acknowledge, but appear munificently to repay), whether there could be better regulations than those which are carried out at the Abattoir of Montmartre. Adieu, my friend, for I am away to the other side of Paris, to the Abattoir of Grenelle! And there I find exactly the same thing on a smaller scale, with the addition of a magnificent Artesian well, and a different sort of conductor, in the person of a neat little woman with neat little eyes, and a neat little voice, who picks her neat little way among the bullocks in a very neat little pair of shoes and stockings.

Such is the Monument of French Folly which a foreigneering people have erected, in a national hatred and antipathy for common counselling wisdom. That wisdom, assembled in the City of London, having distinctly refused, after a debate of three days long, and by a majority of nearly seven to one, to associate itself with any Metropolitan Cattle Market unless it be held in the midst of the City, it follows that we shall lose the inestimable advantages of common counselling protection, and be thrown, for a market, on our own wretched resources. In all human probability we shall thus come, at last, to erect a monument of folly very like this French monument. If that be done, the consequences are obvious. The leather trade will be ruined, by the introduction of American timber, to be manufactured into shoes for the fallen English; the Lord Mayor will be required, by the popular voice, to live entirely on frogs; and both these changes will (how, is not at present quite clear, but certainly somehow or other) fall on that unhappy landed interest which is always being killed, yet is always found to be alive - and kicking.

Brokers' And Marine-Store Shops

When we affirm that brokers' shops are strange places, and that if an authentic history of their contents could be procured, it would furnish many a page of amusement, and many a melancholy tale, it is necessary to explain the class of shops to which we allude. Perhaps when we make use of the term 'Brokers' Shop,' the minds of our readers will at once picture large, handsome warehouses, exhibiting a long perspective of French-polished dining-tables, rosewood chiffoniers, and mahogany wash-hand-stands, with an occasional vista of a four-post bedstead and hangings, and an appropriate foreground of dining-room chairs. Perhaps they will imagine that we mean an humble class of second-hand furniture repositories. Their imagination will then naturally lead them to that street at the back of Long-acre, which is composed almost entirely of brokers' shops; where you walk through groves of deceitful, showy-looking furniture, and where the prospect is occasionally enlivened by a bright red, blue, and yellow hearth-rug, embellished with the pleasing device of a mail-coach at full speed, or a strange animal, supposed to have been originally intended for a dog, with a mass of worsted-work in his mouth, which conjecture has likened to a basket of flowers.

This, by-the-bye, is a tempting article to young wives in the humbler ranks of life, who have a first-floor front to furnish, they are lost in admiration, and hardly know which to admire most. The dog is very beautiful, but they have a dog already on the best tea-tray, and two more on the mantel-piece. Then, there is something so genteel about that mail-coach; and the passengers outside (who are all hat) give it such an air of reality!

The goods here are adapted to the taste, or rather to the means, of cheap purchasers. There are some of the most beautiful LOOKING Pembroke tables that were ever beheld: the wood as green as the trees in the Park, and the leaves almost as certain to fall off in the course of a year. There is also a most extensive assortment of tent and turn-up bedsteads, made of stained wood, and innumerable specimens of that base imposition on society, a sofa bedstead.

A turn-up bedstead is a blunt, honest piece of furniture; it may be slightly disguised with a sham drawer; and sometimes a mad attempt is even made to pass it off for a book-case; ornament it as you will, however, the turn-up bedstead seems to defy disguise, and to insist on having it distinctly understood that he is a turn-up bedstead, and nothing else, that he is indispensably necessary, and that being so useful, he disdains to be ornamental.

How different is the demeanour of a sofa bedstead! Ashamed of its real use, it strives to appear an article of luxury and gentility, an attempt in which it miserably fails. It has neither the respectability of a sofa, nor the virtues of a bed; every man who keeps a sofa bedstead in his house, becomes a party to a wilful and designing fraud, we question whether you could insult him more, than by insinuating that you entertain the least suspicion of its real use.

To return from this digression, we beg to say, that neither of these classes of brokers' shops, forms the subject of this sketch. The shops to which we advert, are immeasurably inferior to those on whose outward appearance we have slightly touched. Our readers must often have observed in some by-street, in a poor neighbourhood, a small dirty shop, exposing for sale the most extraordinary and confused jumble of old, worn-out, wretched articles, that can well be imagined. Our wonder at their ever having been bought, is only to be equalled by our astonishment at the idea of their ever being sold again. On a board, at the side of the door, are placed about twenty books, all odd volumes; and as many wine-glasses, all different patterns; several locks, an old earthenware pan, full of rusty keys; two or three gaudy chimney-ornaments, cracked, of course; the remains of a lustre, without any drops; a round frame like a capital O, which has once held a mirror; a flute, complete with the exception of the middle joint; a pair of curling-irons; and a tinder-box. In front of the shop- window, are ranged some half-dozen high-backed chairs, with spinal complaints and wasted legs; a corner cupboard; two or three very dark mahogany tables with flaps like mathematical problems; some pickle-jars, some surgeons' ditto, with gilt labels and without stoppers; an unframed portrait of some lady who flourished about the beginning of the thirteenth century, by an artist who never flourished at all; an incalculable host of miscellanies of every description, including bottles and cabinets, rags and bones, fenders and street-door knockers, fire-irons, wearing apparel and bedding, a hall-lamp, and a room-door. Imagine, in addition to this incongruous mass, a black doll in a white frock, with two faces, one looking up the street, and the other looking down, swinging over the door; a board with the squeezed-up inscription 'Dealer in marine stores,' in lanky white letters, whose height is strangely out of proportion to their width; and you have before you precisely the kind of shop to which we wish to direct your attention.

Although the same heterogeneous mixture of things will be found at all these places, it is curious to observe how truly and accurately some of the minor articles which are exposed for sale, articles of wearing apparel, for instance, mark the character of the neighbourhood. Take Drury-Lane and Covent-garden for example.

This is essentially a theatrical neighbourhood. There is not a potboy in the vicinity who is not, to a greater or less extent, a dramatic character. The errand-boys and chandler's-shop-keepers' sons, are all stage-struck: they 'gets up' plays in back kitchens hired for the purpose, and will stand before a shop-window for hours, contemplating a great staring portrait of Mr. Somebody or other, of the Royal Coburg Theatre, 'as he appeared in the character of Tongo the Denounced.' The consequence is, that there is not a marine-store shop in the neighbourhood, which does not exhibit for sale some faded articles of dramatic finery, such as three or four pairs of soiled buff boots with turn-over red tops, heretofore worn by a 'fourth robber,' or 'fifth mob;' a pair of rusty broadswords, a few gauntlets, and certain resplendent ornaments, which, if they were yellow instead of white, might be taken for insurance plates of the Sun Fire-office. There are several of these shops in the narrow streets and dirty courts, of which there are so many near the national theatres, and they all have tempting goods of this description, with the addition, perhaps, of a lady's pink dress covered with spangles; white wreaths, stage shoes, and a tiara like a tin lamp reflector. They have been purchased of some wretched supernumeraries, or sixth-rate actors, and are now offered for the benefit of the rising generation, who, on condition of making certain weekly payments, amounting in the whole to about ten times their value, may avail themselves of such desirable bargains.

Let us take a very different quarter, and apply it to the same test. Look at a marine-store dealer's, in that reservoir of dirt, drunkenness, and drabs: thieves, oysters, baked potatoes, and pickled salmon, Ratcliff-highway. Here, the wearing apparel is all nautical. Rough blue jackets, with mother-of-pearl buttons, oil- skin hats, coarse checked shirts, and large canvas trousers that look as if they were made for a pair of bodies instead of a pair of legs, are the staple commodities. Then, there are large bunches of cotton pocket-handkerchiefs, in colour and pattern unlike any one ever saw before, with the exception of those on the backs of the three young ladies without bonnets who passed just now. The furniture is much the same as elsewhere, with the addition of one or two models of ships, and some old prints of naval engagements in still older frames. In the window, are a few compasses, a small tray containing silver watches in clumsy thick cases; and tobacco- boxes, the lid of each ornamented with a ship, or an anchor, or some such trophy. A sailor generally pawns or sells all he has before he has been long ashore, and if he does not, some favoured companion kindly saves him the trouble. In either case, it is an even chance that he afterwards unconsciously repurchases the same things at a higher price than he gave for them at first.

Again: pay a visit with a similar object, to a part of London, as unlike both of these as they are to each other. Cross over to the Surrey side, and look at such shops of this description as are to be found near the King's Bench prison, and in 'the Rules.' How different, and how strikingly illustrative of the decay of some of the unfortunate residents in this part of the metropolis! Imprisonment and neglect have done their work. There is contamination in the profligate denizens of a debtor's prison; old friends have fallen off; the recollection of former prosperity has passed away; and with it all thoughts for the past, all care for the future. First, watches and rings, then cloaks, coats, and all the more expensive articles of dress, have found their way to the pawnbroker's. That miserable resource has failed at last, and the sale of some trifling article at one of these shops, has been the only mode left of raising a shilling or two, to meet the urgent demands of the moment. Dressing-cases and writing-desks, too old to pawn but too good to keep; guns, fishing-rods, musical instruments, all in the same condition; have first been sold, and the sacrifice has been but slightly felt. But hunger must be allayed, and what has already become a habit, is easily resorted to, when an emergency arises. Light articles of clothing, first of the ruined man, then of his wife, at last of their children, even of the youngest, have been parted with, piecemeal. There they are, thrown carelessly together until a purchaser presents himself, old, and patched and repaired, it is true; but the make and materials tell of better days; and the older they are, the greater the misery and destitution of those whom they once adorned.

Making A Night Of It

Damon and Pythias were undoubtedly very good fellows in their way: the former for his extreme readiness to put in special bail for a friend: and the latter for a certain trump-like punctuality in turning up just in the very nick of time, scarcely less remarkable. Many points in their character have, however, grown obsolete. Damons are rather hard to find, in these days of imprisonment for debt (except the sham ones, and they cost half-a-crown); and, as to the Pythiases, the few that have existed in these degenerate times, have had an unfortunate knack of making themselves scarce, at the very moment when their appearance would have been strictly classical. If the actions of these heroes, however, can find no parallel in modern times, their friendship can. We have Damon and Pythias on the one hand. We have Potter and Smithers on the other; and, lest the two last-mentioned names should never have reached the ears of our unenlightened readers, we can do no better than make them acquainted with the owners thereof.

Mr. Thomas Potter, then, was a clerk in the city, and Mr. Robert Smithers was a ditto in the same; their incomes were limited, but their friendship was unbounded. They lived in the same street, walked into town every morning at the same hour, dined at the same slap-bang every day, and revelled in each other's company very night. They were knit together by the closest ties of intimacy and friendship, or, as Mr. Thomas Potter touchingly observed, they were 'thick-and-thin pals, and nothing but it.' There was a spice of romance in Mr. Smithers's disposition, a ray of poetry, a gleam of misery, a sort of consciousness of he didn't exactly know what, coming across him he didn't precisely know why, which stood out in fine relief against the off-hand, dashing, amateur-pickpocket-sort- of-manner, which distinguished Mr. Potter in an eminent degree.

The peculiarity of their respective dispositions, extended itself to their individual costume. Mr. Smithers generally appeared in public in a surtout and shoes, with a narrow black neckerchief and a brown hat, very much turned up at the sides, peculiarities which Mr. Potter wholly eschewed, for it was his ambition to do something in the celebrated 'kiddy' or stage-coach way, and he had even gone so far as to invest capital in the purchase of a rough blue coat with wooden buttons, made upon the fireman's principle, in which, with the addition of a low-crowned, flower-pot-saucer-shaped hat, he had created no inconsiderable sensation at the Albion in Little Russell-street, and divers other places of public and fashionable resort.

Mr. Potter and Mr. Smithers had mutually agreed that, on the receipt of their quarter's salary, they would jointly and in company 'spend the evening', an evident misnomer, the spending applying, as everybody knows, not to the evening itself but to all the money the individual may chance to be possessed of, on the occasion to which reference is made; and they had likewise agreed that, on the evening aforesaid, they would 'make a night of it', an expressive term, implying the borrowing of several hours from to- morrow morning, adding them to the night before, and manufacturing a compound night of the whole.

The quarter-day arrived at last, we say at last, because quarter- days are as eccentric as comets: moving wonderfully quick when you have a good deal to pay, and marvellously slow when you have a little to receive. Mr. Thomas Potter and Mr. Robert Smithers met by appointment to begin the evening with a dinner; and a nice, snug, comfortable dinner they had, consisting of a little procession of four chops and four kidneys, following each other, supported on either side by a pot of the real draught stout, and attended by divers cushions of bread, and wedges of cheese.

When the cloth was removed, Mr. Thomas Potter ordered the waiter to bring in, two goes of his best Scotch whiskey, with warm water and sugar, and a couple of his 'very mildest' Havannahs, which the waiter did. Mr. Thomas Potter mixed his grog, and lighted his cigar; Mr. Robert Smithers did the same; and then, Mr. Thomas Potter jocularly proposed as the first toast, 'the abolition of all offices whatever' (not sinecures, but counting-houses), which was immediately drunk by Mr. Robert Smithers, with enthusiastic applause. So they went on, talking politics, puffing cigars, and sipping whiskey-and-water, until the 'goes', most appropriately so called, were both gone, which Mr. Robert Smithers perceiving, immediately ordered in two more goes of the best Scotch whiskey, and two more of the very mildest Havannahs; and the goes kept coming in, and the mild Havannahs kept going out, until, what with the drinking, and lighting, and puffing, and the stale ashes on the table, and the tallow-grease on the cigars, Mr. Robert Smithers began to doubt the mildness of the Havannahs, and to feel very much as if he had been sitting in a hackney-coach with his back to the horses.

As to Mr. Thomas Potter, he WOULD keep laughing out loud, and volunteering inarticulate declarations that he was 'all right;' in proof of which, he feebly bespoke the evening paper after the next gentleman, but finding it a matter of some difficulty to discover any news in its columns, or to ascertain distinctly whether it had any columns at all, walked slowly out to look for the moon, and, after coming back quite pale with looking up at the sky so long, and attempting to express mirth at Mr. Robert Smithers having fallen asleep, by various galvanic chuckles, laid his head on his arm, and went to sleep also. When he awoke again, Mr. Robert Smithers awoke too, and they both very gravely agreed that it was extremely unwise to eat so many pickled walnuts with the chops, as it was a notorious fact that they always made people queer and sleepy; indeed, if it had not been for the whiskey and cigars, there was no knowing what harm they mightn't have done 'em. So they took some coffee, and after paying the bill, twelve and twopence the dinner, and the odd tenpence for the waiter, thirteen shillings in all, started out on their expedition to manufacture a night.

It was just half-past eight, so they thought they couldn't do better than go at half-price to the slips at the City Theatre, which they did accordingly. Mr. Robert Smithers, who had become extremely poetical after the settlement of the bill, enlivening the walk by informing Mr. Thomas Potter in confidence that he felt an inward presentiment of approaching dissolution, and subsequently embellishing the theatre, by falling asleep with his head and both arms gracefully drooping over the front of the boxes.

Such was the quiet demeanour of the unassuming Smithers, and such were the happy effects of Scotch whiskey and Havannahs on that interesting person! But Mr. Thomas Potter, whose great aim it was to be considered as a 'knowing card,' a 'fast-goer,' and so forth, conducted himself in a very different manner, and commenced going very fast indeed, rather too fast at last, for the patience of the audience to keep pace with him. On his first entry, he contented himself by earnestly calling upon the gentlemen in the gallery to 'flare up,' accompanying the demand with another request, expressive of his wish that they would instantaneously 'form a union,' both which requisitions were responded to, in the manner most in vogue on such occasions.

'Give that dog a bone!' cried one gentleman in his shirt-sleeves.

'Where have you been a having half a pint of intermediate beer?' cried a second. 'Tailor!' screamed a third. 'Barber's clerk!' shouted a fourth. 'Throw him O-VER!' roared a fifth; while numerous voices concurred in desiring Mr. Thomas Potter to 'go home to his mother!' All these taunts Mr. Thomas Potter received with supreme contempt, cocking the low-crowned hat a little more on one side, whenever any reference was made to his personal appearance, and, standing up with his arms a-kimbo, expressing defiance melodramatically.

The overture, to which these various sounds had been an ad libitum accompaniment, concluded, the second piece began, and Mr. Thomas Potter, emboldened by impunity, proceeded to behave in a most unprecedented and outrageous manner. First of all, he imitated the shake of the principal female singer; then, groaned at the blue fire; then, affected to be frightened into convulsions of terror at the appearance of the ghost; and, lastly, not only made a running commentary, in an audible voice, upon the dialogue on the stage, but actually awoke Mr. Robert Smithers, who, hearing his companion making a noise, and having a very indistinct notion where he was, or what was required of him, immediately, by way of imitating a good example, set up the most unearthly, unremitting, and appalling howling that ever audience heard. It was too much. 'Turn them out!' was the general cry. A noise, as of shuffling of feet, and men being knocked up with violence against wainscoting, was heard: a hurried dialogue of 'Come out?' - 'I won't!' - 'You shall!' - 'I shan't!' - 'Give me your card, Sir?' - 'You're a scoundrel, Sir!' and so forth, succeeded. A round of applause betokened the approbation of the audience, and Mr. Robert Smithers and Mr. Thomas Potter found themselves shot with astonishing swiftness into the road, without having had the trouble of once putting foot to ground during the whole progress of their rapid descent.

Mr. Robert Smithers, being constitutionally one of the slow-goers, and having had quite enough of fast-going, in the course of his recent expulsion, to last until the quarter-day then next ensuing at the very least, had no sooner emerged with his companion from the precincts of Milton-street, than he proceeded to indulge in circuitous references to the beauties of sleep, mingled with distant allusions to the propriety of returning to Islington, and testing the influence of their patent Bramahs over the street-door locks to which they respectively belonged. Mr. Thomas Potter, however, was valorous and peremptory. They had come out to make a night of it: and a night must be made. So Mr. Robert Smithers, who was three parts dull, and the other dismal, despairingly assented; and they went into a wine-vaults, to get materials for assisting them in making a night; where they found a good many young ladies, and various old gentlemen, and a plentiful sprinkling of hackney-coachmen and cab-drivers, all drinking and talking together; and Mr. Thomas Potter and Mr. Robert Smithers drank small glasses of brandy, and large glasses of soda, until they began to have a very confused idea, either of things in general, or of anything in particular; and, when they had done treating themselves they began to treat everybody else; and the rest of the entertainment was a confused mixture of heads and heels, black eyes and blue uniforms, mud and gas-lights, thick doors, and stone paving.

Then, as standard novelists expressively inform us, 'all was a blank!' and in the morning the blank was filled up with the words 'STATION-HOUSE,' and the station-house was filled up with Mr. Thomas Potter, Mr. Robert Smithers, and the major part of their wine-vault companions of the preceding night, with a comparatively small portion of clothing of any kind. And it was disclosed at the Police-office, to the indignation of the Bench, and the astonishment of the spectators, how one Robert Smithers, aided and abetted by one Thomas Potter, had knocked down and beaten, in divers streets, at different times, five men, four boys, and three women; how the said Thomas Potter had feloniously obtained possession of five door-knockers, two bell-handles, and a bonnet; how Robert Smithers, his friend, had sworn, at least forty pounds' worth of oaths, at the rate of five shillings apiece; terrified whole streets full of Her Majesty's subjects with awful shrieks and alarms of fire; destroyed the uniforms of five policemen; and committed various other atrocities, too numerous to recapitulate. And the magistrate, after an appropriate reprimand, fined Mr. Thomas Potter and Mr. Thomas Smithers five shillings each, for being, what the law vulgarly terms, drunk; and thirty-four pounds for seventeen assaults at forty shillings a-head, with liberty to speak to the prosecutors.

The prosecutors WERE spoken to, and Messrs. Potter and Smithers lived on credit, for a quarter, as best they might; and, although the prosecutors expressed their readiness to be assaulted twice a week, on the same terms, they have never since been detected in 'making a night of it.'

Charles Dickens - A Short Biography

Charles Dickens (1812-1870) is regarded by many readers and literary critics to be THE major English novelist of the Victorian Age. He is remembered today as the author of a series of weighty novels which have been translated into many languages and promoted to the rank of World Classics. The latter include, but are not limited to, *The Adventures of Oliver Twist*, *A Tale of Two Cities*, *David Copperfield*, *A Christmas Carol*, *Hard Times*, *Great Expectations* and *The Old Curiosity Shop*.

Birth and Childhood's Hardships

By and large, Charles Dickens's life story is one of somebody who is born and raised in dire straits to become one of the greatest men who have marked human history and thought. It is a perfect example of how the plight of the deprived and the destitute could transform into a precious incentive that pushes them to challenge their circumstances and to unexpectedly excel and shine.

Charles Dickens was born in Portsmouth on February 7th, 1812. His father John Dickens worked as a simple accounting clerk at the Naval Pay Office and the family's pecuniary situation was almost always uneven. When Charles was only two years, the family had to move to London, then later to Chatham. For financial reasons, Charles did not have adequate education. He rather had to leave school at a very young age to work at a polishing and blacking factory. To add insult to injury, Charles's father was imprisoned in 1824 after failing to pay a 40-pound debt.

Charles's experience at the factory played a tremendous role in building the novelist's personality and in deepening his concerns about working children and about the working class in general. Dickens's precocious maturity and the serious responsibilities that he had as a little child left a clear impression on many of his young characters, such as Oliver Twist, David Copperfield and Pip in *Great Expectations*. The hardships that Charles Dickens personally went through made him much interested in defending the poor, in fighting social injustice through exposing its blatant manifestations and in accentuating the importance of having decent work conditions.

Between 1824 and 1827, Dickens's father, who eventually managed to pay his debts, offered Charles the opportunity to attend a private school in North London, the Wellington House Academy. The experience surely enriched the young man's knowledge of the rules of writing and rhetoric and whetted his appetite for 18th-century novels and for the picaresque novels that adorned his father's library. However, during this period, Charles still had to experience another disappointment when his mother refused to spare him the strenuous job at the blacking factory even after the relative improvement of the family's financial situation. The mother's decision had a great psychological impact on young Charles and even influenced his vision of gender roles as he thought that the mother should not be the decision-maker in the family.

Early Publications

Young Charles Dickens occupied numerous jobs and worked hard to learn shorthand. This long and diversified professional experience had a patent impact on his different writings. Indeed, after the blacking factory experience, Dickens first worked as a clerk for attorneys, which allowed him to learn about the legal system and its principles, to become a free-lance reporter for Doctor's Commons Courts in 1829. Later, he even wrote reports for the House of Commons before starting to work for newspapers, magazines and journals.

It was in 1833 that Dickens started writing short stories for a number of literary magazines and journals such as *The Monthly Magazine.* A collection of these texts was later pseudonymously published under the title *Sketches by Boz*. Thanks to Dickens's humor and exceptional writing style, the latter publication was relatively successful, but not as successful as *The Pickwick Papers* whose serial publication sold thousands of copies and raised Dickens to considerable fame. In 1836, he started writing short texts to be published with the humorous illustrations of the famous artist Robert Seymour. These first successes encouraged Dickens to carry on publishing other stories in the form of series. Dickens's next creation was *Oliver Twist* which was published between 1837 and 1839.

It is noteworthy that most of Dickens's novels were published in the form of monthly and weekly chapters which, according to critics and biographers, allowed him to evaluate and adjust his characterizations and plots to meet the expectations of his readership. It was also during this period that Dickens started his long career as a literary magazine editor.

Loves and Marriage

Charles Dickens got married on April 2nd, 1836 to Catherine Thomson Hogarth after one year of engagement. They settled at the famous Furnival's Inn in Holborn, London, before they moved to their home in Bloomsbury. The house was transformed into the Charles Dickens Museum in 1925. Charles and Catherine, who lived there with the first three of their ten children, were joined by Charles's brother Frederick and Catherine's sister Mary. The latter was reported to have had a very special place in Charles's heart. After dying in his own arms in 1837 following a sudden illness, she became a source of inspiration for some of his female characters. After three years of marriage, Dickens's success and rising income made him leave the house for larger and more luxurious estates.

Catherine Hogarth was not Dickens's only love, however. Indeed, biographers report that Dickens's relation with his wife was sandwiched by two other romantic affairs. First, there was Maria Beadnell, a banker's daughter, with whom Dickens fell in love when he was only eighteen years old. The relationship ended three years later when Maria's parents apparently intervened. The other love story that Dickens went through started in 1857 and pushed him to divorce Catherine the following year. It was when Dickens was having a group of young actresses for the staging of his play *The Frozen Deep* that he fell in love with the actress Ellen Ternan who was 27 years younger than him.

Major Achievements

Charles's first success with *The Pickwick Papers* and *Oliver Twist* only pushed him to devote more time and energy to his writing and editorial activities. After publishing *Nicholas Nickleby* between 1838 and 1839, he started a new project in 1840 that he entitled *Master Humphrey's Clock*. The latter is a collection of stories that share the same frame and have recurring characters. It was among this collection that the two major works *The Old Curiosity Shop* and *Barnaby Rudge* were serially published.

After visiting the United States of America in 1842, Dickens developed a rather negative view of the New World which was mainly depicted in his travelogue *American Notes for General Circulation* and also in his picaresque novel *Martin Chuzzlewit*. The latter included very harsh satire of the republic and strongly denounced its institution of slavery. However, the fury that Dickens caused among some American circles was soon quietened with the publication of *A Christmas Carol* in 1843. The book, which is considered by many as the novelist's finest opus, was celebrated both in England and America.

Two other Christmas books followed respectively in 1834 and 1845. They are *The Chimes* and *The Cricket on the Hearth*. During this period, Dickens also published a new travelogue that he entitled *Pictures from Italy* following his stay in the Mediterranean country. Another Christmas story entitled *The Haunted Man* was published in 1848, which was preceded by *Dombey and Son* (1847) and *The Battle of Life* (1847) and followed by David Copperfield (1849-1850), *Bleak House* (1852-1853) and *Hard Times* (1854).

It was in 1853 that Dickens started organizing public performances in which he presented his literary works. By this time, he also started to collaborate with Wilkie Collins on a number of short stories and plays. *Little Dorrit* started as a monthly serial in 1855 to be finished in 1857. Later, two of Dickens's most valuable works were published: *A Tale of Two Cities* (1859) and *Great Expectations* (1861). They were both published in the weekly periodical, *All the Year Round*, which he founded and edited himself.

Apart from his writings, Dickens's main profitable activity was the public reading of his novels. Along with the money he earned thanks to his successful publications, public readings allowed Dickens to buy his dream house (Gad's Hill Place, Kent), to offer financial help to his parents and brothers and to engage in charitable activities.

Twilight and Death

During the 1860s, Dickens carried on organizing more reading tours. In addition to the many events he had in England, he visited France, the United States, Scotland and Ireland on many an occasion. In 1864, he started his last complete novel, *Our Mutual Friend*. However, by 1865, his health started to waver. This was mainly because of the physical and intellectual exhaustion to which he subjected himself. Furthermore, Dickens was psychologically traumatized in 1865 following a train crash.

He was with his beloved Ellen Ternan on their way back from Paris when their train derailed to cause a big number of casualties. Although Dickens was able to collect his courage and managed to help the wounded and comfort them, the picture of the disaster affected him greatly and could never be erased from his mind.

For health reasons, Dickens cancelled many of his programmed readings between 1868 and 1870. On April 22nd, 1869, he had a stroke. The latter was followed by a second stroke on June 8th, 1870, while he was working on his novel *The Mystery of Edwin Drood* which would remain unfinished. The next day, he passed away. Charles Dickens today rests in The Poets' Corner of Westminster Abbey.

www.ingramcontent.com/pod-product-compliance
Lightning Source LLC
Chambersburg PA
CBHW061458170626
46811CB00004B/1573